T0064005

The Way of the Warrior

The Way of the Warrior

Includes the Shaman, Tara and the Demon Slayer

Kathiresan Ramachanderam

PARTRIDGE

A Penguin Random House Company

To order additional copies of this book, contact
Partridge India
000 800 10062 62
orders.india@partridgepublishing.com

www.partridgepublishing.com/india

Contents

This book is dedicated to Dyarne who has been the light that has never ceased to shine in my darkest hour, to my mum and dad for their kindness and devotion, to my sis, brother in law and the kids for their endless support and to Cherie, Rudi and the girls.

Preface

"Having indulged in the light of the glorious sun, I the warrior priest see the ultimate truth in all its forms and manifestations and I understand that he who commands is the all auspicious one, the Brahmatma who is the light of the spiritual world. The Brahmatma protects, safeguards, confers and withdraws all benefits. I take the reins of my flock, my group, my kingdom in a manner so that they may observe and witness the radiance and the glory of the supreme soul. I do this alone" – Book of Warriors

At the height of the Empire a period which scholars commonly refer to as the Golden Age of the Empire, the teachings of the sects were at their peak and schools were constructed in every corner of the Empire. Students enrolled in these schools after the completion of their training as priests. The ages of the pupils varied, depending on how quickly they grasped the principles of religious doctrines and established covenants and upon completion of their training they acquired the title "warrior priests".

The most important prerequisite for the warrior priest is to gain the ability to absolve himself from the karmic consequences that follow the act of killing. All kills attract karmic reprisals and the warrior must be aware of the principle of action and reaction.

Therefore in order to avoid the court of Maya and to avoid the journey through the sixteen cities that the soul passes through upon its death dragged by a noose around its head by the emissaries of the Death God, the warrior has to first and foremost navigate through the labyrinth that is karma.

Karma is like a dark cloud that stalks its victim and the unfortunate soul that has not repented or has not erased the sins that it has committed during its lifetime will be subjected to punishment many times more intense than the crime it has committed. The pain is excruciating.

Therefore it is only prudent, where possible, to erase the sin that is brought about as the result of the act of killing prior to committing the act. To those who worship their chosen God or Goddess diligently and conduct their affairs in accordance with religious principles Maya will appear as a God of noble countenance. To others he will appear in his most terrifying form.

At the onset of this book it must be made clear that karmic sins are never completely erased but they can be mitigated by charitable acts. Therefore the warrior must act in accordance with the principle that for every life he takes he must save at least a hundred lives. A warrior may kill a single man but the act of killing that one man may save an entire city and its population. Therefore the sin of killing is mitigated considerably and the retribution that follows in accordance with karmic law is limited to the barest minimum.

The astute warrior will realize that good karma negates bad karma and it is in his interest to accrue as much good karma as possible. The following will help the warrior acquire good karma: - sympathy towards all living beings, pleasant conversation, belief in a supreme religion, helping others, truthfulness, wholesome advice to others, belief in the authority of the religious texts, devotion to the preceptors, angels, celestial beings and divine sages, association with good men and women, eagerness in performing noble deeds and friendship. By balancing good karma with bad karma the warrior will be able to avoid or at the very least reduce the repercussions that result from the act of killing.

Karma is the arc nemesis of all warriors. Bad karma is like a noxious gas that escapes into the atmosphere when the kill is made. Like an invisible cloud it is released from the victim's body at the time of death. If the victim is of a pervasive nature than the karma that is released is not so lethal. Otherwise it is deadly.

Victims who have accrued merits or have repeatedly performed charitable deeds release virulent karma which is both malicious and malevolent at the time of the kill. The killing of sages, hermits and priests are the most precarious and it is reserved only for those higher up in the echelon.

Negative karma stalks its prey. It has form and definable characteristics. Like a shape shifter it has the ability to change its shape at will. Malignant by design it seeks to mete out punishment by any means necessary.

The warrior priest must be well versed with the nature and substance of the Brahmatma or the super soul in order to evade the negative karma that stalks him after he has made the kill. It suffices to say that the Brahmatma is the source of all things, good and evil, and he is the past, the present and the future. In short he is existence.

All schools teach that death is best bestowed between twilight and sunrise, from the hour of the setting sun when the world is subdued by the hazy pale of orange to the time when Shamash sets the sky alight astride his golden chariot pulled by solar steeds.

It is the time of day when spirits and demons lurk around every obscure corner and when the great wheel of justice descends into the night only to be reborn the following morning. It is the time when most victims are least able to resist, their minds and bodies in a weakened state.

There are eight common ways of bringing about death. The way of manifold blades and arrows, the way of animals, the way of crushed flesh, the excellent way of suffocation, the way of cleaver implements, the way of plants, the way of divine intervention and the slow path of disease.

The Way of Manifold Blades and Arrows

The way of manifold blades and arrows is subtle yet profound. All blades have their uses. It is the most suitable path for the warrior and it includes incisive thrusts to the correct nerve centers with knifes, bent knifes, swords, daggers, spears and arrows.

Therefore the warrior priest needs to acquire an understanding of the human body and needs to know with certainty the exact location of each nerve centre. Mastering this technique involves a two pronged approach. In addition to being able to identify the nerve centers in the body, the warrior must also diligently learn the art of swordplay, archery and acquire sufficient skills to stab with knifes, swords, daggers and other sharp implements.

The warrior may become embroiled or entangled in a situation where he does not have a sword, a knife or a dagger on hand and therefore he must be versatile enough to fashion a sharp implement from wood, glass, metal or any other substance or material that may be available to him at the time in order to defend himself. Mastery of this art has saved many a warrior in desperate times.

The basic sword of the warrior and the most widely used throughout the Empire is the straight bladed sword. It has three components. There is the grip, the guard and the blade which narrows to the point. Additional components may include a pommel which is located at the head of the grip. It is sometimes used for decorative purposes. The pommel and the grip are collectively referred to as the hilt of the sword.

The next type of blade that is common in the Empire is the saber. The hilt of the saber is located at the pinnacle of a curved blade. The saber is divided into nine parts. The hilt is divided between a grip and a guard that goes around the fingers to prevent it from being severed during battle.

The uppermost portion of the blade is called a mouthpiece; follow by a segment of the blade commonly referred to as the upper hook. Subsequent to that there is the lower hook and the most prominent part of the blade is referred to as the body. Right at the bottom after the toe of the sword is the scabbard point.

Next to swords the most common blades in the Empire are daggers. Warriors must keep in mind that while daggers sometimes resemble a miniature sword or saber (daggers like swords can be divided between straight blades and curved blades) the parts are labeled differently.

The top part of the dagger is often referred to as the hilt, grip or handle and daggers unlike narrow bladed swords do not have a pommel. Below the hilt or the grip there is a metal bar suitably located between the blade and the handle. The bar is called a cross guard or a quillion.

In addition to narrow or straight bladed daggers, curved bladed daggers are also common in the Empire. Curved bladed daggers are commonly called kukris. They are single sided blades with the razor sharp edge located on the downward pointing part of the blade. The toe or the point of the blade is called the tip. The part of the blade just below the hilt is called the notch. The hilt of the blade is divided into three parts the grip, the shaft and the chapro.

In addition to acquiring proficiency with the blade the warrior must also be adept with an arrow. The kill cannot always be made at close range or proximity and the warrior is sometimes required to make the kill from a distance.

Bows of the Empire are made of white oak that is obtained from the northern sector located in the outer reaches of the Empire. Bow makers divide the bow into eight components. The wooden portion of the bow comprises of the upper limb which is located at the top arch of the bow. It is followed by the sight window, which is located in the middle and just below the sight window is a grooved grip crafted for ease of handling. The bottom arc of the bow is called the lower limb.

The bow string is made of cord. The ends of the string are attached to the string groove located at both ends of the bow and right in the middle opposite the sight window is the nocking point. Just below that is the serving. This is the most common type of bow crafted and used in the Empire and it varies in size and length.

A bow needs the right arrow. Arrows are divided into four components, the head which is the most deadly part of the arrow, followed by the shaft normally shaped from thin durable wood. The top end is attached to the arrow head and feathers are attached to the bottom end of the shaft; a little slit is made at the lower tip. It is called the nock and it fits perfectly into the bowstring.

Arrow heads and blades are laced with poison to hasten the kill. Poisoned implements are crucial for the assassin who normally operates clad in black, in the dead of the night.

The aforementioned blades are deadly in the hands of a master but mastery requires time and practice. Be warned, it is unwise to kill without reason and it is most prudent to kill as an act of punishment for a crime or an offence that has been committed. The karmic reprisals are lessened by the victim's own misdeeds. With the exception of a dual or a battle, this is when the warrior will be doing most of his killing.

If a simple crime is to be punished it is usually enough to cut off the extremity that committed it. It is customary if possible to strike at the nerve that is responsible for the crime. For those who are overly dominated by lustful and base desires a thrust is made to the groin, for greedy and gluttonous people a thrust is made to their navel. People who firmly deny their true emotions and corrupt their leadership with ambition should be struck in the solar plexus. Prideful thinkers and fools who have used their thoughts to serve baser desires are struck in the heart.

People who have misunderstood the higher principles of life are commonly beheaded. This is the most common punishment for deviant priests. If the kill is to be made without the pomp and pageantry of beheadings, it is best to just severe the jugular.

People who extend their life-force to the detriment of others, or even drain others of their life-force, are struck in the pineal gland. Finally, those few who have corrupted their true self are struck above the head so that their existence will be forever obliterated.

The Way of Animals

Nature is our greatest teacher. It is required of warriors who follow this path to learn the subtle nuances of each animal. Some paths require extensive preparation and are more complicated or more demanding than others.

The way of animals includes, to name a few, the path of the lion, the path of the leopard, the path of the tiger, the crushing path of the enraged elephant, the cleaver ripping of monkeys, the plunge of the hawk, the path of the snake and the mythical path of the unicorn.

The list is endless and the warrior once he understands the nature or temperament of the animal he selects will emulate its characteristics. Most warriors do not restrict themselves and opt to replicate the traits of more than one animal. Masters of this path may merge the attributes of two or more animals to create a blend or a fusion that is unique to them.

The warrior may choose an unconventional path for example the path of the buffalo suitable for those who display a higher degree of persistency or the path of the jackal, a most heinous and deadly path, suitable for assassins.

The paths of the lion, leopard and tiger are all suitable for virtuous warriors, great hunters and young men. It is a path for those with zest and zeal; for those who are valiant by nature. It is by essence an aggressive path.

The enraged path of the lion is suitable for warriors who display an air of nobility. Warriors who follow this path remain calm and are unruffled by the events that transpire around them. They are strong, vibrant and have little or no need for subtlety.

The way of the leopard is suitable for warriors who are sleek, cunning and extremely intelligent. These warriors are more reliant on speed and grace than power.

The path of the tiger is suitable for warriors who are boisterous and energetic and exude elegance in their approach. Warriors that follow this path are unpredictable and have a tendency to react in the least anticipated manner.

The crushing path of the enraged elephant is commonly used by warriors whose deliberate movements ooze confidence and are calm in all aspects of their life. It is a path that is adopted by veterans who have been in battles on numerous occasions. It is a combination of unwavering commitment and wisdom garnered from years of experience. Warriors that follow this path are slow to anger but do have a tendency to display a violent temper.

The clever ripping of monkeys is reserved for warriors who are versatile, resourceful and tenacious. Warriors who follow this path attack in a highly unorthodox manner.

The plunge of the hawk is the highest of paths suitable for those who have acquired the mantle of leadership. The hawk never fears or falters when its keen sight has spotted its prey. It swoops without warning, sinking its razor sharp talons into its victim without a moment's hesitation. It results in the cleanest and purest kills that often resemble a masterpiece or a masterstroke.

The path of the snake involves many twists and turns and the warrior learns not only the skill to attack but to evade. Often in a dual or a battle the warrior must learn to avoid the onslaught of an opponent. Indeed it is common for warriors to make comparisons on the merits of their kills. Kills that are made in accordance with the stipulations of the laws of karma are rated higher than others.

The path of the unicorn is suitable only for spiritual men. In the months when the skies are right, the horned stallion leaps from star to star covered in stardust. It is a rare path, and often requires carefully selected prayers to succeed but it is most rewarding because when the unicorn opens the heart of a man his soul will follow the spiral of its horn into the light thus seeing the world as it is. It is a path of wisdom for when the unicorn shines its light, followers of this path will be liberated.

The Way of Crushed Flesh

As for the way of crushed flesh it must be said that pain is a cleansing sensation that will purify the soul. The way of crushed flesh is often regarded as base and simple but its merits are undeniable. The most common path in the way of crushed flesh is the path of falling rocks.

It is a simple yet exquisite path since rocks can be suitably concealed. A common practice is to hide above a narrow pass, a building or a ruin and wait. This path is most suitable for ambushes of cavalcades that traverse narrow valleys. The warrior will learn the value of patience for it may be a long wait before the enemy arrives. It is most suitable for small units who wish to bring about the demise of larger contingents.

The path of clubs: Ah yes! The club is the oldest weapon in existence but despite the passage of time it has repeatedly proved its worth. Nothing knocks sense into an enemy like being battered with a club. Warriors must however be aware that the club like the blade requires much skill and mastery of the club is as difficult as mastery of the blade. A lot depends on the size of the club. It goes without saying that the bigger the club the more strength that is required to wield it and that explains why most warriors prefer or rather proficiency with the blade.

The path of high cliffs: This path is deemed suitable for enemies of the Empire especially spies and convert operatives who seek to reveal the secrets of the noble institution. The perpetrators are blindfolded and bound with ropes before being led to the edge of a cliff where they are thrown down together with the riches that they have accumulated as a result of their treachery.

The Excellent Way
of Suffocation

The excellent way of suffocation: This path is divided into the path of locked hands and the path of ropes. All schools teach the path of locked hands but it is hard to do for many. It is known that the grip has to be firm and remind the user of a heart. The path of locked hands requires a vice like hold around the victim's throat. Death is swift and merciful.

The path of locked hands in addition to strangling the victim can be deployed to deliver a lethal blow which is often more effective than an untrained punch with closed fists. Much depends on where the blow is delivered, to the neck, to the heart or to the groin. One blow is sufficient to render the victim unconscious and in most cases it results in death.

Killing to the uninitiated is an art that requires many hours of practice and the warrior must not fail to comprehend the elegance of it. Some warriors even go to the extent of wearing make-up into battle and their appearance can be most deceiving. It often takes the enemy by surprise and they realize their mistake only after the lethal stroke or the deadly blow has been delivered. Therefore it is wise not to underestimate an opponent no matter how unassuming he may look.

The path of ropes: This path has many twists and turns and it is most confusing to the untrained. At times vine stems can be twisted to form a rope and at other times materials such as the fibrous bark of trees, coconut hair, camel hair, horse hair, thongs of sinew or cut hides from animals, cotton, jute, sisal, flax and wild hemp can be spun together to produce a rope. The rope is then used to strangle the victim. Some warriors do not use ropes but opt instead for pieces of cloth.

The best way to strangle a victim is to approach him from the rear, but masters have strangled from all directions, even hanging from a branch above. The victim is normally unaware of the attack until it is too late and will doubtlessly struggle.

The warrior can create a loop, similar to a hangman's noose or something less complicated depending on the warrior's expertise which of course matures with age and lasso his victim. Ideally the noose should encircle the neck but beginners tend to make the mistake of throwing the noose around the upper body which results in an unnecessary struggle.

The excellent way of suffocation is most suitable for the assassin and the master of this path can bring about death with the flimsiest cord. An accomplished assassin schooled in the subtle and coarse ways of touch can choke his victim without leaving a trace.

The Way of Clever Implements

The way of clever implements involves mechanical traps and devices used to ensnare the victim. Traps are suitable for dealing with those who seek the warrior out of curiosity, hate or misunderstanding. They are commonly divided into falling traps, traps that open, traps that strike and traps that change.

Traps can be built by using an assortment of items such as wood, sharp implements, ropes etc. Warriors are encouraged to exploit their creative skills when building a trap.

A simple but effective trap common among hunters is a snare trap. A looped piece of string is hidden on the ground and covered with leaves, twigs and branches. One end of the string or cord is attached to the branch of a young sapling. The branch has to be able to bend but should not break or snap under stress. Therefore this method is more suitable for small animals.

The other end of the string is attached to a piece of wood and the first piece of wood like the upper arm is adjoined to the second piece of wood or lower arm by an elbow mechanism. The looped piece of string is attached to the second piece of wood or lower wood and buried just beneath the surface of the ground. This overly simplistic approach yields poor results and warriors are encouraged to devise their own traps or enhance existing modules.

Another common method of snaring the victim is to hide a piece of string just beneath the surface and to attach both ends of the string to poles on either side. A little lever holds the string to the ground and when the unsuspecting hoof or foot treads on the lever the string springs up and brings the victim or the animal down. It is a mechanism that is commonly used throughout the Empire.

This is followed by an old favorite, the method of digging a hole in the ground and filling it with spikes. The hole is covered with leaves and the surface of the trap is camouflaged. This method is painstaking, especially for warriors who usually display an adversity to shovels but nonetheless effective.

Further improvisations can be made to the lever mechanism and sharp spikes can be attached to a long branch and hid among tall bushes. When the lever is triggered it releases the branch which springs at the unsuspecting victim. It is a most inspiring way of bringing about a kill. Further improvisations can be made to the lever or maybe it is more appropriate to say the trigger method and can also be applied to the path of falling rocks.

It is essential for the warrior to distinguish between the way of the hunter and the way of the warrior. The hunter sets his traps to snare his prey while the warrior sets his traps to exterminate his enemy. There is some correlation between the both in that the mechanisms employed are deviously similar. But if the hunter is cunning the warrior needs to be infinitely more cunning and his implements must bring about swift death.

The way of clever implements also includes sharp blades that are attached to the arm beneath the sleeves, the toe of the boot or the apparel that the warrior has on him. Such implements yet again work on the lever principle and often take the enemy by surprise. It becomes crucial in close combats especially when the combatants are evenly matched.

The more blades the warrior has hidden on his body the higher the rate of success. The assassin also deploys a similar strategy and it becomes increasingly more relevant to the assassin because the assassin is always in a situation where he needs to make a quick getaway or an escape and hidden weapons facilitate this escape.

In order to construct the right mechanism or trap the warrior needs to be familiar with wood, string, metal and a range of materials that go along with trap making.

The Way of Plants

The way of plants: This way is most often used for assassinations of artisans, merchants, landowners and warriors. The way of plants is divided into seven paths; the way of deadly essence, the trickery of food, the way of weighted possessions, the dark bride, the noxious fruits of the valley, the path of spiked demons and the garden of the Goddess.

The way of deadly essence: This is the simplest path. Extracts from bright yellow flowers of the Empire are prepared with freshly churned butter or ghee and then given to the victim. Many schools know of other mixtures to use and improvise on the concoctions. Extracts from plants like castor, belladonna, rosary pea, wolfsbane, water hemlock, yew, strychnine, angel's trumpet, doll's eyes and white snakeroot make deadly poisons.

The trickery of food: This is a most popular path because it is simple to learn and often it is best used when the recipient is not intended to know the sender of the gift. By participating in the cooking of the food, either poison or decay can be hidden beneath its lovely taste, killing or sickening the eater. The aforementioned poisons would suit the purpose ideally.

The way of weighted possessions: This is a more subtle path, where the possessions of the victim are poisoned by smearing them with the essence of powerful plants. A beautiful variation is to curse the possessions so that greedy people will be struck while virtuous people will remain safe.

The dark bride: This way was discovered by a rival aristocrat when he sought to end the reign of a prince. He gave a lovely maiden ten cups of the dark plant to drink, praying to the Goddess to strengthen her body and fill her with the force of the waning moon. He then sent the girl to the prince, who was delighted by her beauty and scent. As he kissed her in the palace garden, the prince fell down dead.

The noxious fruits of valleys: The fruits of valleys and hills have many wondrous properties. They are dark, like rotten grapes, but smell of sandalwood and hide beneath leaves like outstretched hands. Interestingly these fruits give the eater vivid sights that are more realistic than that of the real world and often terrifying as they reveal his innermost fears. The eater can then be approached and admonished properly, often realizing his guilt to the extent that he voluntarily accepts death. This method is commonly used against liars.

The path of spiked demons: This path is secret, only known to the masters. It involves the spiked demons of the sea, who will willingly reveal the whereabouts of potent poisons growing in the undersea gardens. These poisons are powerful and unknown to all but the master mixers.

The garden of the Goddess: There is a classic preparation, often used for worthy or dangerous opponents. Rare flowers and leaves are gathered and their petals placed on the altar of the Goddess. The leaves are cut, crushed and rolled with paper.

The warrior then smokes the leaves and enters the sleep of visions to visit the garden of the Goddess, beyond the sacred mountain. In the garden, he prays to the Goddess for guidance using the three high verses and in the name of her eternal beauty requests that she provides him with a drop of demon blood belonging to the demons that were vanquished in the battle before time.

If the master of plants is found to be worthy, the Goddess will appear and give him a drop of the blood. It is then given to the victim, usually mixed with food and the deadly delights of the garden of the Goddess will be his.

The Way of Divine Intervention

The path of divine intervention: This is the path of power. This path involves death that is brought about by unnatural or holy means and should not be taken lightly. Abusing this path may mean that the Gods themselves may wish to bestow the gift of death on the warrior.

This is not the path of the mage or the sorcerer, the wizard or the warlock. It is the path of the sage or the hermit, the path of the master who falls at the feet of the mountain mendicant, from whose matted dreadlocks swerving rivers flow. It is the path of he who is clothed in feral leopard skins, who is naked to the waist and who wields the trident of power. It is one of the numerous paths of Zhiva.

To use this path the warrior must undergo intense preparations and must confront the dead. It begins with the warrior isolating himself in a graveyard or an abandoned battlefield, the latter is more suitable, because of the horrific deaths that it has witnessed. The remnants of blood and corpses that have seeped into the ground defile the land to the extent that it is no longer suitable for consecration. Amidst the remains of the once sordid scenes, dark specters lurk around every corner and the apparitions become more active as the hours dwindle and night approaches.

Grossly disfigured, scarred beyond comparison they circumvent the world of the living and the dead and navigate between the both, trapped in limbo until such time as the emissaries of the Death God Maya deem it fit to release them from the torturous void.

The warrior may have encountered many deaths in his time and therefore may not be put off by the sight of death or the remains of grossly mutilated bodies but rest assured witnessing what lingers after death is much worse. It is indeed the truest test of courage.

All warriors are encouraged to undergo a period of self imposed exile in the sacred grounds of the dead to witness the results of their handiwork and one who has witnessed the true brutality of death and the remains of the victim that return after death is worthy of being conferred the title master.

After a prolonged period of meditation and feeding on wild plants and herbs growing on a ground enriched by the decomposing corpses of the dead and if the mountain mendicant deems fit, he allows the warrior to spy on his most auspicious countenance and bestows upon him a boon.

The Slow Path of Disease

This is a common way of orchestrating the death of many and what might be difficult to do in a battlefield can easily be done by culturing the right pathogens and releasing the harmful bacteria in the air or into the water. It is however prudent to first have an antidote on hand. Common diseases like smallpox, dysentery, measles, leprosy, typhus, fever and syphilis can be conjured and concocted in an enclosed environment before being released into the air.

If the intended victim has been unusually nefarious it is not unnatural for the warrior to turn to unspiritual means to teach the victim a lesson in etiquette and good behavior. This can be done by summoning spirits that travel in the air. These spirits are malicious but not demonic in essence.

Pazuzu, a spirit that is associated with the southwesterly wind brings with him plagues during the dry season and locusts during the rainy season. He is a spirit of dubious intent but reliable when it comes to unleashing fevers, boils and other ailments on the victim.

Epilogue

Warriors of the Empire upon completion of their training are dubbed warrior priests. Having acquired proficiency in both the sacred verses and having developed the knack to kill, they are free to experiment and find new and innovative methods to bring about the demise of the enemy. Needless to say the means of doing so are endless.

———◇———

The Shaman

I have for the past two decades been an ardent connoisseur of the paranormal and in that time I have come to the conclusion that spirits do exist and they do without doubt linger and on certain occasions possess. It is a phenomenon that we are not all that familiar with and it is an area that we are just beginning to understand. Our knowledge of the spirit world is at its infancy and we are only now starting to grasp its fundamentals.

To a warrior in the olden days the assistance of shamans and spirits was much sought after. Before we go any further it is essential that we draw a distinction between help from spirits and spiritual help. The latter refers to divinities and the former refers to help from spirits that have failed or refused to cross over.

It is also best to distinguish between cases of possession and alternate personalities that appear under hypnosis beforehand. It is my belief that the human mind is divided into two components, the conscious mind and the subconscious mind.

I base my argument on the premise that the subconscious minds of all persons are linked and when the physical body is in a state of comatose or deep sleep the conscious mind ceases to be active and the subconscious mind takes control.

The subconscious minds of all persons are connected to a collective consciousness called the super consciousness that stores all memories past, present and future. Therefore the mind of one person is able to access the memories of another and hence one person is able to assume the personality of another under hypnosis.

Similarly the subconscious mind is able to travel vast distances and traverse regions never before explored when the body is in deep sleep. This phenomenon is called the outer body experience. It is essential to differentiate between the outer body experience and normal dreams. Normal dreams are visions that we have during sleep. In most instances it is a culmination of the stresses or dilemmas that we encounter during the day and often we wake up without suffering any aftereffects.

The outer body experience is much more intense and the soul, which is the life-force of the body or the engine that drives the body, is flung thousands if not millions of miles away and the body wakes up drained and tired, sagging from the experience. These dreams also at times reveal the future and are precognitive.

I am of the opinion that the super consciousness, this collective repository that is the past, the present and the future is God, who according to ancient Vedic texts resides or is the fourth dimension.

Therefore anyone who is able to stimulate a nexus with the fourth dimension, the dimension of the super soul, I refer to the super soul as the Brahmatma, can transgress the space time continuum and see into the past or look into future.

Having dismissed cases of alternate personalities that manifest under hypnosis as not being cases of actual possession but merely the sharing of memories and setting aside the possibility that possession may be a sickness of the mind the only other probable conclusion that I can come too is that there are indeed spirits that may seek to possess others.

Death is a universal experience but customs and traditions with regards to it differ from culture to culture. According to the Tibetan Book of the Dead (Bardo Thödol), the mourning period for the departed is forty nine days. During that period the body slowly falls away and at the end only the soul which is the size of the thumb remains. The soul after it has left the body is in a state of confusion and therefore needs to be coaxed into making the journey to the next life. The Bardo Thödol was composed by the Indian monk Padmasambhava in the 7th century and was condensed into writing by his student and disciple Yeshe Tsogyal.

I am also going to draw a distinction between spirits and souls. Spirits are beings that still retain their human form and the soul is what remains when that human form gradually falls away or disappears.

Upon death, the spirit is confronted by a series of wrathful deities or Bardo visions and if the spirit is able to dismiss these visions as simple manifestations emanating from the conscious mind like the Buddha did when he meditated under the Bodhi tree then at the end of the forty nine days the soul will attain liberation. If however the spirit cannot distinguish between reality and the projections of a lingering consciousness, the spirit will be relegated once again to the karmic cycle of birth and death.

For Hindu's the mourning period is three hundred and sixty five point two days during which time the spirit crosses sixteen cities before it finally arrives for adjudication in the court of Yama. The God of Death is the knower of all truths.

Not all spirits cross over willingly and some are adamant and wish to remain. These are the spirits that have a higher propensity to possess. While modern science attributes sudden changes in a person's behavioral pattern to unknown illnesses of the mind and further compounds the problem by prescribing drugs and other medications, reputable and renowned psychoanalysts remain convinced that there are other reasons, not found in schools of accepted science but in the unobtrusive and inconspicuous field of occultism. Occultism may sometimes be defined as the religion behind all religions.

The original faith of the Tibetan people, the Bon religion, is a realization and an admittance that we share this world with other entities, some visible and some not. Ancient but not obsolete, it is a faith that's still practiced, handed down through the generations, often merged with Hinduism and Buddhism. It is propitiation by means of incantation.

It is the appeasement of spirits in return for their aid or assistance. In reality the Bon practitioner or shaman is worth more in monetary terms than the humble and honest monk who seeks to shepherd his flock down the path of righteousness because while the good shepherd cannot bestow wealth and riches or bring about the sudden demise of an enemy or produce a miracle cure for an ailment, these men and women can. It is a faith that is Tantric in nature without the frills of covenants or adherents. Central to Bon is the yungdrung. It is the key to unlocking the door to the other world.

Bon is similar to Altaic shamanism. It is the faith of communion with spirits, conjured or invoked for answers and solutions.

Peculiar to the Altai shaman is the horse sacrifice. It is a representation of the importance that is attached to the horse by the Altai people. Its significance leads me to the conclusion that the original inhabitants of the Altai were pastoral nomadic tribes with a close nexus to the tribes that first inhabited the Kazakh Steppe. According to the Greek historian Heorodtus, the Scythians started to branch out of the Kazakh Steppe at about 1,000 B.C. These are the most likely forefathers of the Altai nation.

Hence when the Altai shaman makes a sacrifice to appease the spirits, he slaughters the animal he values most, the horse, as the highest form of offering to his chosen spirits. This to some degree explains the horse sacrifice. It is a reflection of the cultural heritage that these shamans share with the pastoral nomadic tribes that first ventured into the region.

Altai shamans, especially during public exhibitions, mime or mimic the movement upwards in a rite or a passage that is often more dramatic than ecstatic, for example a horse that rises above to the sky to capture the attention of their audience. It is more symbolic and has little tangible value but it also represents the shaman's ascension of the shaman tree, a requirement that needs to be satisfied before acquiring shamanhood.

This certainly does not mean that Altai shamans are incapable of trances. It is only that these occur at other shamanic séances. For the warrior who has acquired the skills of a shaman slipping in and out of the trance state is crucial to achieving victory.

The word shaman is derived from the Tungusic word šaman. A shaman is someone who performs religious ceremonies and is capable of seeing what others cannot i.e. spirits and the gods of the cosmos.

The shaman's inner vision gives him sight of things and cosmic events that cannot be explained. Shamans further develop the ability to communicate with both good and malicious spirits but in practice they choose either one or the other and it is impossible to find a neutral shaman simply because the spirits that they are in contact with aren't.

The ability to communicate with spirits and cosmic beings gives them the capacity to perform miracles, foretell the future and perform all the other functions commonly related to shamans.

The primitive faith of the Altai people is called Turanism. It has existed for eons and all known religions have a touch of Turanism in their equation or composition. It is Tantric, shamanic, paganistic and ritualistic in practice and it works for all those who adhere to its principles.

Turanism is based on the realization that there are other entities that inhabit the same time and space as mortals, endowed, gifted or blessed with magical and mystical abilities.

Turanism attempts to bond with these supernatural and ultra natural beings. It is a faith without a codified identity and it is a faith that is communalistic, isolated and restricted to specific localities, often handed down from teacher to disciple or from father to son.

The shaman is the cardinal and principle figure in the Turan faith. There is no prescribed mode of worship and much is dependent on the spirit that the shaman is in contact with. It is to some degree the worship of nature and the elements.

It is not unknown for followers of the Turan faith to worship trees, rocks, and other objects. Semblance of the being that is worshipped is a question of perception and perception differs from person to person, from village to village and from tribe to tribe.

Turanism is similar to animism from the perspective that all entities, animate and inanimate possess a spiritual quality and therefore are worthy of worship.

Turan priests and shamans commune and speak to spirits, at times allowing the spirit to take control or possess the body of the shaman during rituals. This can also be classified as induced possession i.e. when the shaman willingly allows the spirit to occupy his body and it's a ritual that is practiced to this very day.

Chanting in the Turan faith is central to worship and it is often accompanied by the beat of drums, enabling the

Turan priest or shaman to drift into self induced hypnosis during which time the spirit takes control of the priest or the shaman's body.

The chants are guttural and often rhythmic, at times chanted loudly to be audible enough to the onlookers and at other times whispered in silence. Worship is sometimes accompanied by sacrificial offerings, the act of feeding or appeasing the spirit or spirits, and the sacrificial object is often an animal. The type of animal depends on the spirit that's being summoned but human sacrifice is not unheard off. The assistance of spirits is dependent on gifting it with the elixir of life, blood.

Other forms of Turanic worship include the use of boards similar to ouija boards, bones of dead animals, and even seashells. The Shaman as a result of his loyalty and devotion is gifted with foresight and clairvoyance and this is exceptionally important during battles.

The shaman can also perform miracles, cure illnesses, grant good fortune, arrange fortuitous marriages and forge stoic alliances. Turanic texts are few and far apart and the knowledge is rarely shared because the success of the shaman is linked to his ability to control the spirit that he is in contact with. Therefore it is a ritual that is best kept unknown.

Turanism is sometimes split into fictitious divisions of white and black magic. The categories are nonexistent in the shamanic context because the rites and rituals are the same. It is categorized as white magic when it brings about a good turn of events and black magic when it results in the opposite. Yet again it's a question of perception.

Shamanic believes are elemental, deeply rooted and firmly connected to the land. Inanimate objects like stones and idols do not possess spiritual matter, but there is a rite, an ancient ritual, that breathes life into an inanimate object and infuses it with spiritual matter.

The spirit is housed within the inanimate object, for example a slab of stone and repeated chanting and offerings especially of blood, over time, strengthens the power of the spirit within the object.

The size of the object is irreverent, and often little trinkets can possess great power. The age of the object is relevant. The older it is, the higher the likelihood that it has been infused with spiritual matter and hence it is unwise to purchase an idol or a good luck charm that looks antique without knowing a bit about its history. Shaman warriors usually have little trinkets around their necks, wrists or hips.

As attractive as some of these trinkets may look they may have been subjected to shamanic rites or rituals and they can either bestow good fortune or misfortune on the bearer or wearer. In the same manner, spiritual essence can be infused into weapons like swords and daggers to make them invincible. Such idols, trinkets and weapons are best restricted to places of worship.

Certain areas or localities have a higher presence of spiritual matter than others and that's due to the practices of the initial people who lived, toiled and tilled the land. People die and turn to dust, spiritual matter doesn't and it long outlives its followers. There is a way of freeing the spirit and returning it back to the source but it is by no means easy and a lot depends on the spells that were used to bind the spirit in the first place. Shamanic texts aren't much help even if they were available because they are often intelligible and need deciphering.

Not everyone can become a shaman and it is achieved after subjecting the body to severe and rigorous hardships. Shamanism is acquired, whether natural or induced, at the point of death, and this can be brought about by a severe illness or by undertaking austere penances.

A shaman according to all the accounts given by sources from the northern hemisphere becomes aware of his shaman tree after a prolonged or a life threatening illness and he acquires his shamanic powers after this near fatal episode.

The near death experience opens the channel to the spirit world and following the near fatality, the shaman tree that is relevant to him (each shaman has his own tree) is revealed to the shaman. It becomes visible or apparent at the point of death or at the time the spirit is about to leave the body.

In short the aspiring shaman must have come as close to death as possible, if only for a few seconds. One prescribed method of subjecting the body to the near death experience is by fasting. Fasting is not a sin and if things go wrong the participant does not attract the karmic reprisals that are usually equated with suicide.

At the time of death the body will find itself being lifted, it doesn't sink, but has the feeling of floating higher towards a white light. This feeling of climbing higher is the feeling or sensation of ascending the shaman tree and it is only possible in a state of comatose or deep sleep when all else has become numb and the limbs are struck by temporary paralysis.

Once the body has undergone this stage it will, to start with, be able to feel if not see spirits and the new shaman has to harness the bond with his spirit and his spirit tree. Initially he will experience a phenomenon that is commonly referred to as a visitation. The visitations will continue and gradually the spirit will reveal itself to him.

In the early stages he will be able to see footprints, dark imprints on the floor as the spirit approaches him and as time goes by he will be able to see its whole body.

The spirit resides in the shaman's tree and depending on his aptitude he can invite more than one spirit to reside in his tree. The most common way of appeasing these spirits is with animal sacrifices. The shaman tree is unique by itself and peculiar to the shaman.

In Siberian shamanic circles chopping down a shaman's tree is said to result in the death of the shaman. In Altaic circles a deceased shaman would customarily be entombed in the hollow of a deciduous tree. In the narrative poetry of the Yakutians (a Siberian ethnic group), the top of the tree serves as a hitching post for the highest God. The importance of the tree to the shaman is clearly evident and the tree continues to exist long after the death of the shaman.

In certain cultures the shaman upon death is entombed within the tree. The tree is worshipped after the death of the shaman and continues to grant minor miracles. Ritual sacrifices or offerings of blood if permissible within the community will only strengthen the spirit of the tree.

So just exactly who or what are these external spirits that form the core of shamanism? The answer in short is that, the spirits shamans confer with are the spirits of those who have died but haven't yet crossed over to the afterlife.

Between death and the hereafter there is a transitory stage that the soul has to pass through before it is completely freed from the shackles of mortal existence. During this stage the soul retains its physical appearance and it is not bereft of its senses. These are the spirits that shamans commune with.

The spirit will look exactly like it did just before its last breath left its body and the spirit of someone who died on a battlefield will appear to the shaman complete with the scars and wounds that eventually led to his or her death. The shaman sees the exact replica of the person seconds before the passing.

Having retained the ability to communicate, the spirit can now converse with the shaman but only in the language that it knows or that is stored in its consciousness. Death doesn't increase the spirits linguistic capabilities but it does acquire certain other abilities that are useful to the shaman.

Therefore an Altai spirit will only be able to converse in the Altaic language, a Burat spirit will only be able to converse in the Burat language and a Yakut spirit will only be able to converse in the Yakut language.

In the trance state the shaman merges with the spirit that he has acquired. The pure trance state is a state of sheer ecstasy where the shaman loses himself and the spirit takes complete control, not unlike the transformation that comes over the legendary berserker, who suddenly metamorphoses from a normal man to become a lethal warrior.

There was a time, according to folklore, when shamans acquired the ability to transgress the space between the mortal world and the heavens and go beyond. They journeyed to infinite locations in their trance state. The ancient traditions give details of when shamans flew into the clouds, and were able to ride on the solar boat as it sailed across the sky gracing the earth with sunshine. Shamanism is probably the oldest universally practiced religion in the world and every culture of antiquity, before the advent of modern religion has adopted some variant of it.

The Tamang shamans of Nepal and the Tungus shamans after going through the near death experience can see spirits, not visible to others and they can speak or communicate with these spirits.

In contemporary circles testimonies from those who have survived near death experiences confirm the aforementioned principle. Accounts of white lights and sightings of spirits in white after regaining consciousness are numerous.

The recollections of those who have managed to survive the near death episode fits perfectly with all descriptions of the outer body experience. The soul is separated from the body temporarily and during this interim period the soul is flung thousands if not millions of miles from the body.

Possession

It is relevant at this stage to distinguish between possession (someone who is possessed by spirits) and someone who functions with the aid of spirits. The shaman belongs in the latter category and he remains in control with his faculties intact.

Possession in normal terms refers to a physical and psychological state where the body is inhabited by a foreign entity, in most cases, the spirit of a deceased. Possession can be divided into two categories, firstly where the other personality appears only when it is prompted for example during a séance or during the induced trance state and the second category of possession is when the spirit appears without warning (this is sometimes put down as a mental illness).

I am going to dismiss the first category of possession as not actual possession because some measure of control remains firmly in the hands of the shaman.

The second type of possession is the more extreme of the two and it is generally limited to those who live in rural communities. This may denote a link between possession and other factors like environment, living conditions, rites and religious customs.

In most instances the alternate personality that appears is so wholly and substantially different from the person that normally occupies the body that there is no conceivable explanation for the transformation.

Possession in general is more frequent among women and young adults and this is most likely the result of a weaker disposition. Someone who is timid is a more suitable candidate for haunting spirits than someone who is brave and resolute. According to exorcists who coincidentally occupy a position in all religions, there are different categories of spirits that can possess the body and the success of the exorcism is dependent on the strength of the spirit that has occupied the body. In some cases it is not possible to rid the body of the offending spirit.

In cases of actual possessions, the victim is sometimes able to remember the time when the spirit entered the body. In the case of a young girl who suddenly displayed signs of hysteria, speaking in a different voice and exhibiting the physical strength of someone many times her age, she remembered walking past a tree alone, when she suddenly took fright and saw a dark light beside the tree. Days later, she went into sudden hysterics, while at school, waving her arms wildly and speaking in the voice of a much older person. The case occurred in the 1960's in a rural town.

The teachers fortunately were not unfamiliar with such cases of possessions and applied an old wives remedy that is allegedly supposed to rid the body of unwanted guests.

They took a pinch of dry chili powder and pressed it on the girl's toenail. When they pressed down on the toenail with the chili powder, the girl began to scream. Such an exercise would not have had any effect on a normal person but in cases of mild possessions, the haunting spirit is known to feel pain. They kept applying the pressure on the toenail with the chili powder until the girl, having exhausted herself from screaming, fainted.

Despite the intervention of orthodox religious covenants, these rituals continue to exist and the church itself does not deny the possibility of possession. The bible clearly tells us, where there is a body; there is a soul or a spirit.

Possession is by virtue a difficult proposition. The symptoms are classic and the victim displays strength many times that of his or her age. The victim often goes into hysterics. In one case the victim's tongue, was for many hours drawn like a semi-circle up to the roof of her mouth. The victim may start ranting and raving and often what the victim says is in stark contrast to the victim's normal temperament.

Spirits give shamans a keener sense of perception and increase his strength and at times endurance, manifold. It influences both his body and his senses, taking his abilities to higher levels.

The Spirit

The body is divided into two components the physical component and the soulful component. Upon death the soul remains encased in the body and goes through a transitory period where it is trapped between the mortal world and the hereafter and remains in the astral world.

The remnants of the body only falls away after the soul has completed the migratory stage. Therefore shamans who are in touch with spirits will be able to clearly see the body with its shape because the spirits that they communicate with are spirits that are trapped between two worlds and still retain, depending on the nature of their deaths, their physical appearance.

During its stay in the facility that is referred to as the astral world i.e. the space between the world of the living and the afterlife, the spirit is not bereft of its faculties and therefore it is still able to see and hear as it did when it was alive. It is invisible to most people but clearly visible to the shaman. The spirit or spirits that the shaman is in contact with become a part of his family.

Spirits that have not crossed over or are stuck in the astral world retain their ability to think, reason and progress.

These spirits therefore have the capacity to evolve. Close scrutiny will reveal that the intellectual properties of spirits vary and that variation is dependent on the abilities of the spirit or the knowledge that it accumulated while it was alive and remains stored in its consciousness. Not all spirits are intelligent and a prudent shaman seeks the services of an astute spirit capable of enhancing his own abilities. Spirits are beings of varying grades of intelligence.

The next question that comes to mind is can an inferior spirit attain the capabilities of a higher spirit? This puts forward an interesting proposition. According to some schools spirits that do not cross over (it appears that they do have a choice after death) can evolve or go up the ladder, much like a person matures from being a child to becoming an adult and his ability to learn and reason matures during the process.

Like all beings that grow the spirit requires sustenance and hence in order for the spirit to evolve it has to be fed and this is one of the prime reasons why shamans perform the rite of sacrifice, to enable the spirit to grow and become stronger. The spirit that the shaman nurtures will continue to exist in its spirit form long after the shaman's death.

In most cases the shaman hands over the care of his spirit or spirits to another shaman just prior to death. If he doesn't the spirit or spirits will continue to linger until they find a new owner or occupant. This little principle will explain why some areas or localities are more accident prone than others.

The spirit that resides there needs to feed and in the absence of regular sacrifices the spirit has to manipulate things in order to satisfy its cravings or its feeding desires. Just like hunger leads men to do the unthinkable, in extreme cases cannibalism, hunger equally leads spirits to precipitate the deaths of others.

In addition to that spirits of those that haven't crossed over are sometimes preoccupied with mortal thoughts and like most people they seek companionship. Their desires are no different to that of the living and are attainable or achievable.

The primary requirements for a shaman's spirit are food, shelter and sometimes companionship. In reality it is no different from the requirements of the living. Hence it becomes the duty of the shaman to satisfy the needs of the spirit or spirits in return for their aid.

Spirits that do not choose to cross over are absorbed into a spirit hierarchy, a spirit world that exists between the third dimension and the fourth dimension. Here they develop and grow stronger as they continue to progress up the hierarchy. To those that have sight of spirits it becomes evident that the dead spend time building their presence under the guidance of these spirit hierarchies.

Spirits that do not crossover continue to develop their own latent abilities. As the spirit rises in the hierarchy it becomes increasingly more powerful and if the shaman is fortunate enough to be in contact with a spirit or spirits higher up in the echelon then he will be granted greater power than most.

Sometimes when there is a conflict between shamans and it is bound to happen, that conflict extents to the spirits that guide the opposing shamans. The spirit that is more powerful will usually be victorious. Therefore it is in the interest of the shaman to ensure that the spirit or spirits that he is in contact with move higher up the hierarchy.

It is not uncommon to hear people speak of shrines that are not dedicated to Gods but spirits located in rural areas or in the interior of forests that do not house any known deity. These shrines are normally there for years, some are even hundreds of years old. It is not uncommon for a person to approach these isolated shrines to request for aid or assistance or to have their boons or wishes granted.

It is a deal or a bargain an individual strikes with a spirit, without the help of a shaman and in return for the spirits assistance it is given a sacrifice; a simple deal that sometimes has far reaching consequences.

The spirit hierarchy is segregated by the elements. There are in actuality five elements, earth, wind, fire, water and aether. Aether the fifth element is spirit and it is a combination of white matter and dark matter.

The most common spirits that shamans come in contact with are earthly spirits or spirits related to the earth. Most people perish or meet their demise on land and therefore roam close to the vicinity of their deaths. Spirits of the dead that have refused to cross over either linger close to their place of death or close to their loved ones and this is clearly evident in cases of suicides and murders.

Slavic myth offers some insights on water spirits. Water spirits are called ruslakas and they are the returning spirits of women who die prematurely or unnaturally close to waterways. The spirits of these women continue to haunt the areas close to water. Rusalkas are sometimes depicted as part fish part women much like mermaids and they are categorized as being the children of lakes and rivers.

I have only heard of fire spirits in Thailand and according to myth they move like tiny fireballs in the dead of the night, after twilight, much like fireflies and linger until dawn. Spirits of the air are more akin to celestial beings. On the more sinister front according to mortal perceptions they personify demonic characteristics.

Tara

The humble supplicant was blessed to spy upon the countenance of the auspicious Goddess. Beaming with curiosity, his face glowing with joy, he asked her "tell me most revered Goddess of your beginnings". The Goddess her voice as sweet as a lark, resonating peace and goodwill, spoke thus "I set foot on this world a millennia ago".....

The demons after performing strict penance and austere worship gained the confidence of the most generous and most gracious Brahma. The munificent lord, pleased with their piety granted them the boons of their request. Blessed with guile beyond mortal comprehension, the crafty demons, requested that they be granted immunity from death in the hands of any known God and that they be bequeathed dominion over all seas and oceans and all creatures living within the folds of vast watery expanses, power surpassing that of even Varuna, the God of the Sea.

The benignant deity complied with their wishes and bestowed upon them the boon that they so desperately sought. Having achieved their purposes and intoxicated with power beyond measure, the demons sought to reignite the age old battle with the Gods and they reached down to the depths of the abyss and summoned legions of the fallen who had been evicted by Indra and the other guardians of heaven for inciting and leading a rebellion against the rulers of heaven.

They successfully unlocked the gates of the abyss and humanity was given a choice, to either replace the worship of Gods with the worship of demons or die. Those who agreed were spared while those who refused came to a most gruesome end, tortured to death by beings bereft of sanity. Sages and holy men were the first to go followed by kings, aryas and ksatriyas.

The monks lit the altars and made offerings of milk, ghee and honey summoning the most sapient of Gods, Agni, God of Fire, cherished messenger of the Gods. They made offerings of sweet meats and performed animal sacrifices, repeatedly chanting mantras and reciting hymns in favor of their selected deities. The priests chanted endlessly in places of worship repeating their mantras with force and the echoes of their chants reverberated for miles around. Devotees thronged to the temples in numbers and fell to their knees praying for mercy and clemency. Their prayers spiraled upwards and soon reached the Guardian of Heaven, Indra.

The God of rain and thunder, armed with the Indraastra, sat astride his winged white elephant and descended from the sky above ready to battle the demons. Assured of his prowess in war the mighty thunderer took to the primeval ocean, his face aglow with confidence. He and Airavata, the mythical elephant soon set foot on the shores of the primeval waters and Indra yelled out jeering at the demons to come forth to do battle.

Awakened by the taunts, the demons rose from the depths of the ocean where they rested, to the surface, the rays of Shamash glistening off the drops of water that was clearly visible on their sleek slithery bodies. Indra released the Indraastra and spates of unrelenting arrows fell from the sky, like torrential rain, coming down on the demons at the rate of knots. Unaffected by the onslaught and shielded by the boon that they had received, they stood their ground and soon broke into inexorable laughter, mocking the God of Heaven. The battle raged for days before Indra finally relented and abandoned all hopes of victory.

The defeated Indra returned to the heavens in retreat and conferred with the elements, Bhumi (Goddess of the Earth), Jala and Varuna (Gods of Rivers and Oceans), Vayu, (God of Air and Wind), Agni (God of Fire) and Shunya (God of Aether). Angered by Indra's defeat, the elements raged.

Bhumi made the earth tremble with the Bhaumastra, Jala and Varuna, discharged un-mitigating volumes of water with the Varunaastra, Vayu let loose strong winds from all eight directions, Agni released the Agniastra, a weapon that emitted inextinguishable torrents of flames and Shuyna leveled the oceans with the force of aether.

The waves of the ocean rose thousands of feet up in the air, its water twisting and swirling and the ground below cracked open. The demons were allowed neither rest nor reprieve. Angered by the continuous and prolonged attack, the demons rushed to a frenzied defense, rampantly repealing the elements, un-dented and unfazed by the assault. Their faculties intact, they retaliated without remorse and outdid the gods with sheer savagery pounding away at them without respite. They battered away at the elements, and crushed the onslaught. The elements bruised and battered, retreated and sought refuge in the skies above.

The angry demons, their fury unquenched and with the lust for victory seeping into every nook and cranny in their body decided it was time to hold the human race ransom. The demons churned the waters of the ocean, turning it into deadly poison and its color transformed from its normal colorless shade and assumed a cool, suave blue, the poison deceptively hidden beneath the elegant tint.

The vanquished Gods, humbled by the defeat, journeyed to the abode of the mountain mendicant, and begged him for assistance. Varuna, God of Seas and Oceans had lost governance of water and was now a God without a domain. The people were in despair. No longer could they touch the waters of streams and rivers, and many succumbed to the toxic venom that filled the waterways. The benevolent Shiva, moved by the pleas of the people and the appeals of the deities, sat astride the white bull of heaven, Nandi, and left his abode atop Mt. Kailash in search of the sinister demons.

When he arrived on the shores of the endless ocean, the auspicious trident wielding God was greeted by a shimmering blue hue that floated on the surface of the water forming a thin toxic layer that stretched for as far as the eye could see.

Concerned for the safety of humanity, Shiva consumed the waters of the endless ocean without leaving behind a single drop. The poisoned water recycled in his belly and his pale white skin was darkened by the lingering residue. The mighty God spat the recycled water out after removing the poison in his belly and the endless ocean was yet again filled with pure water. What remained of the poison became salt and the dense molecules sank to the bottom of the ocean filling the vast watery expanse with saline liquid.

The God with the matted dreadlocks sank unceremoniously to his knees overcome by the severity of the poison, weakened by its effects. The demons sensing victory burst into goading laughter.

Shakti the female incarnation of Shiva, who dwelled in her abode atop Mt. Meru grew alarmed at the unexpected turn of fate that had befallen her consort. Aware that the demons cannot be defeated by a known God, Shakti who epitomized the power of female divinity summoned the collective powers of creation from the void between the created and the uncreated. With their blessings, Shakti manifested herself into a new avatar, Tara, the Goddess of mercy, clemency, kindness and compassion.

Tall, fair of skin, pale of features, with eyes as blue as the ocean and hair as black as a raven's feathers she appeared. She held a sword in her right hand and a shield in the left. She was slim, petite and of mature age. Her weapons were forged from the molten lava that flowed beneath the craters of Mt. Meru. Armed with the sword of seven splendors and the indestructible shield of heaven she boldly ventured forth.

Dressed in flowing white gowns, Tara left the realm of the uncreated and set foot on the earth. Gifted with the unlimited knowledge of Gayathri and Saraswathy, she journeyed to the shores of the endless ocean and there she found Shiva, weak and drained, on his knees, as the poison slipped into his cosmic being, its deadly effects clearly visible.

The Goddess of mercy and clemency lifted the mountain mendicant, and carried him to a nearby monastery and there with help of sages and sagacious disciples of the God Dhanvantari, the God of Ayurvedic medicine, she nursed him back to health.

She placed her lips on his while Shiva lay flat on his back, almost unconscious and she sucked the poison out of his body and absorbed it into hers. The poison was neutralized but its essence lingered and his body remained tainted with a tinge of dark blue, as enigmatic and as mysterious as its owner.

Having restored the benevolent trident wielder back to health and after draining the malevolent poison from his body, the Goddess with the raven hair and eyes of blue sapphire went forward to battle the demons.

As the pale white of her feet touched the golden sandy shores of the endless ocean a breeze blew across the sea and her loose silken garments danced to its invisible touch.

The elements fell downwards from the heavens and knelt in deference on one knee in front of her, their heads bowed down in servitude. Their hands held out, they offered the Goddess their indestructible cosmic weapons to aid her in her quest to slay the spiteful demons.

The Goddess accepted graciously and thanked them not with words. Instead she fixed them with a loving glare that said more than any word could muster.

The Goddess reached out with her infinite mind and summoned the seven splendors whose shrines rested at the foot of Mt. Meru. The feminine divinities left their abodes and journeyed with the wind to the shores of the primeval ocean and there they appeared in human form; female in essence, maternal in instinct and protective by nature.

Clad in loose silken white garments, tall, slim and petite, the women mirrored their mistress in all aspects but their features. They uttered the customary greeting in the manner befitting a Goddess before transforming themselves back to their spiritual form and merging with the sword of seven splendors. Charity, Chastity, Diligence, Humility, Kindness, Patience and Temperance were their names and they were the seven virtues of the sword of seven splendors.

Shamash climbed to the highest point in heaven, and from its pinnacle, he emitted rays of light and wisdom. The zest for battle sped through the limbs of the Goddess and dispersed in all directions. The white of her eyes transformed to the red of rage that spread all over her body shrouding her pale flawless skin with a crimson cover, at the sight of the bluish water.

The oceans churned and the waves grew higher. Propelled by strong winds they rushed at the Goddess at immense speed striking her at a velocity that would instantly tear a normal man asunder.

The Goddess stood her ground bearing the brunt of the assault and withstood the ferocious attack that was fuelled by the relentless wind. She was battered repeatedly by a barrage of tidal waves until the day turned to night and Shamash the sun made way for Chandra the moon. Darkness filled the sky and it was lit only by a pale lunar light. The stars had scurried away to the closest retreat unable to witness the mammoth battle that was about to unfold below.

The demons grew restless, irked by the unmovable Goddess who refused to budge. They convened the council of war. Assured by the boon that they had been granted, the demons made their way to the surface, ready to reduce the unknown divinity to rubble and crush her within the folds of their hands. The lead demon, Tiamat, secure in the knowledge of her immortality, reached out to clench the Goddess with a grip of her mighty fist, but Tara, moved swiftly avoiding her reach and with one swift stroke of her sword severed the hand from the body.

The demon howled in pain, its voice shattering the night sky; stunned that the boon had failed. Shock numbed its body and deprived of its mental faculties; it stood rooted to the ground. In that brief moment of indecisiveness Tiamat met her doom. The Goddess unleashed the Indraastra and spates of unrelenting arrows fell from the sky like torrential rain. No longer was the demon immune from the jagged edges of raining arrows for standing before it was an unknown Goddess and the celestial weapon became deadly in her hands.

The demon was reduced to a corpse within minutes and Tara released the Agniastra. The unremitting flame consumed the carcass reducing it to ashes within the blink of an eye. The merciful Goddess had preformed the death rite even for the wicked demon.

The other demons rushed to avenge their comrades and surged at the Goddess but the mighty Tara fought valiantly cutting and hacking away ruthlessly at her wretched foes until there were none left. She completed her task just as dawn crept over the horizon. Victory complete her skin lost its reddish hue and assumed its normal saintly pale. Having attained victory and rid the world of the demons, the Goddess retreated to Mt. Meru.

"That is how I first set foot on this world most sagacious monk" she said when she had finished. The monk his thirst for knowledge unquenched, pressed for more "Tell me most benevolent of Goddesses, what happened next". The Goddess smiled in her all enchanting manner and continued ….

I roamed the world endlessly for what seemed like an eternity. I was a new manifestation and not yet worthy of representation. I had the eternal knowledge of all Goddesses, but I was not yet able to decipher that knowledge. I was a Goddess in a world of a thousand Goddesses and thus I sought to unravel the wisdom within me. I journeyed to the foot of the Himalayas and there I petitioned the father of the mountains, Maha Rishi Markendaya to look propitiously upon me and to grant me the favor of shaping the deluge within me.

The noble ruler of the Himalayas agreed to my petition and there I remained for a thousand years, in a secluded monastery, isolated in the company of my seven companions. There I sought to unravel the mysteries of the ages. In time my fame spread as did my wisdom and people came to worship me. Temples and monasteries were built in my name and they revered me like they did all their other deities.

In the thousandth year on earth, I had mastered one tenth of the knowledge within the Tantric sphere and the father of the Himalayas conferred upon me the title Mahavidya. I became one of the ten keepers of Tantric wisdom. We are but one in essence but divided in the knowledge that we retain.

In the same year I reinvented myself. I realized that men were frail and their actions were compelled by their fears. One deity did not suffice to alleviate their trepidations. I remodeled myself as Arya - Tara and the prefix in my name is a reminder to all men to constantly strife to maintain the purity of their self and the sanctity of their deeds. I manifested myself in twenty one different forms to alleviate the fears of men. I changed the color of my skin to correspond with the twenty one manifestations I had chosen.

The principle shade of my skin is green and in this form I am the mother of all Taras. It is from this form that the twenty one other manifestations of Tara emancipate. When men worship me in this form they worship all my manifestations and they seek enlightenment and liberation from the wretched lives that they lead, from the disease and decay of a decadent society. They seek to free themselves from corruption and depravation, and from the many sufferings that they endure.

In this form I am motherly and the personification of mercy and clemency. In this form I do not bestow but merely salvage. In this form I ease the suffering of all men guiding them to a placid and meaningful existence.

When the shade of my body turns scarlet I am the personification of courage, the embodiment of Kurukulla, the slayer of demons, the whip that is used to castigate malignant spirits; the dispeller of all evil.

When the shade of my body turns white, I am the personification of mercy and compassion, the embodiment of Sarawathy, the granter of knowledge and wisdom, the companion of the ill and the diseased.

When the shade of my body turns a bluish yellow, I am the personification of virtue, the embodiment of Durga, the guardian of chastity. I am worshipped in this manner by those who have turned away from the material world and seek the path of enlightenment.

When the shade of my body turns white, I am the personification of victory and the embodiment of Lakshmi reflecting the sixteen measures of success:- knowledge, intelligence, strength, valor, beauty, victory, fame, ambition, morality, gold, food, bliss, happiness, health, longevity, and progeny.

When the shade of my body turns reddish yellow, I am the personification of intelligence and the embodiment of Gayathri reflecting the wit of an eternity.

When the shade of my body turns blood red, I am the personification of valor and the embodiment of Chandi reflecting the prowess of creation.

When the shade of my body turns black, I am the personification of victory and the embodiment of Kali reflecting the courage of the demon slayer.

When the shade of my body turns reddish black, I am the personification of victory and the embodiment of Chandi and Kali, the ruthless crushers of all evil.

When the shade of my body turns bluish white, I am the personification of forests, trees, woods and glens, the embodiment of Narayani the guardian of all life forms.

When the shade of my body turns crimson, I am again the personification and embodiment of Durga, the conqueror of the three worlds.

When the shade of my body turns gold, I am the personification of wealth and the embodiment of Kuberan, the giver of untold fortunes.

When the shade of my body turns saffron, I am the personification of auspiciousness and the embodiment of Ishwari, reflecting the propitious qualities of the Goddesses.

When the shade of my body turns ruby, I am the personification of fire, the embodiment of Agni, the bearer of flames.

When the shade of my body turns reddish black, I am the personification of wrath, the embodiment of Virabhadra, symbolizing the vengeance of the destroyer.

When the shade of my body turns pale, I am the personification of peace, the embodiment of Adithi, exemplifying the serenity of nature.

When the shade of my body turns the color of the sun, I am the personification of life, the embodiment of Shamash, demonstrating the energy of the solar deity.

When the shade of my body turns amber, I am the personification of fire, the embodiment of Rudra and the world trembles at my feet.

When the shade of my body turns a placid white, I am the personification of the holy sage, the embodiment of the mountain mendicant and the usurper of all poisons.

When the shade of my body turns a dreamy white, I am the personification of Maya, the representation of the great enchantress and the dispeller of illusions.

When the shade of my body turns a snowy white, I am the personification of peace, epitomizing Parvati, the eliminator of conflicts and bad dreams.

These most holy monk are my twenty one personifications. The monk bowed his head in humility. "Thank you wise and venerated Goddess" he replied. Satisfied he closed his eyes and fell into eternal slumber.

———⊰❖⊱———

The Demon Slayer

The Demon Slayer

"Well?" Babhūti asked. The old woman remained silent, bowing her head in meek acquiescence, "it was but an illness, noble king" she replied. Babhūti frowned. The Gods had once again deemed it fit not to grant him a child. He and his wife had married twenty years ago, at a time when his kingdom was besieged by mercenaries on the payroll of enemy agents.

"It is a wise arrangement, my lord" his ministers had consoled him. "Her prowess in controlling the elements, will secure your state" they said. "You priority is to you kingdom, Babhūti" the former queen, his mother, had told him sternly. If the truth be told he wasn't averse to marrying her at all. She was slim, pretty, pale of skin with long golden hair and eyes as blue as the ocean. They had her tested of course, to see if she was pure. Three different doctors were summoned and each confirmed the findings of the other. "She remains untouched, my lord" they concurred. The matter was settled and they married in a manner befitting a king.

She was different unlike any other woman he had ever met before. She was a dakini and her soul was deeply entwined with the elements. She was blessed with the gift of clairvoyance and if the truth be told he fell in love with her the moment he saw her.

She ensured that the harvest was bountiful and that his coffers were filled to the brim. She had managed to keep his enemies at bay and despite the exorbitant tax that was levied on his kingdom, peace prevailed and the people were happy. There wasn't much more Babhūti could ask for with the exception of a male heir.

She looked at herself in the mirror and forced a gentle smile at the reflection that appeared on the immaculate white glass. "Was it too much to ask for a child?" she pondered. Her marriage was decided for her and she had been fortunate enough to find a loving husband. It was all a woman could want. Yet she felt incomplete and her maternal instincts craved for a child. A woman was never fully satisfied until she became a mother.

Her room was filled with mirrors of all shapes and sizes. It was not due her vanity but to reflect the objects of her summoning, a means to reach out to the elements and the other dakinis who skillfully manipulated the world. She stepped away from the mirrors and walked towards the balcony. She pushed back the long silken, hand embroidered curtains, and threw open its glass doors. She walked out on to the verandah and looked at the full moon that lit the night sky. The hour was close to midnight, the hour of bewitchment and enchantment; the hour of summoning the Goddess Varahi, the Goddess of all Dakinis.

Of the Goddess there is little to be said. She wore the face of a boar. It was she who had lifted the world from the depths of the primeval waters with her huge tusks, long before man had set foot on the earth. Feared, revered and largely misunderstood, she is the most auspicious of all Goddesses. She was the Goddess not only of the dakinis but the Goddess preceptor of all seers. She sat on the fifth chakra; untouched and unperturbed by the chaos that besieged the world, summoned only by those to whom she had granted the privilege of summoning her.

The queen turned and walked towards the center of the room. She sat down and assumed the full lotus position, her loose cotton garments fluttered in the gentle breeze that blew in through the open glass doors. Her head held high, she faced the moonlit sky and repeated the sacred verses that summoned Varahi.

She chanted in rhythmic harmony and as she continued her melodic recital a gentle fog wafted through. It gathered at the entrance of the glass doors and soon resembled a soft white cloud.

"Come in" welcomed the queen and the cloud drifted in until it was a foot away from her. She fell silent and watched the cloud take shape and transform into a ravishing young lady. A sultry seductive woman, with long flowing hair, pale blue eyes, lips succulent and alluring, as red as the petals of a rose, her cheekbones high and haughty, appeared.

The scent of wild jasmines filled the air when she approached. She was tall and broad shouldered her frame lean and feminine, her breasts luscious and rounded and her shoulders slimmed to a petite waist. Her hair danced in the breeze like the flames of a wooden fire.

Her sultry aura emanated a calm radiance, soothing to the soul and her appearance was most pleasing to the eye. Anyone could have fallen instantly in love with her until they looked into her eyes. They were as sharp and as piercing as that of a raging hawk, predatory, with an instinctive desire to kill.

The goddess who is normally depicted with the head of a boar, the all auspicious Goddess of white and black magic, stood in front of the queen. "Welcome mother" greeted the dakini. The Goddess smiled and sat, her legs crossed, in front of the queen. She looked at the dakini, her face filled with compassion. She reached out and gently touched her on the cheek. "Fret not precious one," she said.

"I know that it is a child that you crave for and it is a child that you will have. I will gift you with a child that fears neither man nor demon, a child that has walked the eight million four hundred thousand precincts of hell without fear and has scoffed at the guardian of the abyss" "The enemies of your husband, who even as we speak conspire to transgress the borders of his kingdom will know darkness the likes of which they have never felt before. He will swallow them, engulf them, and they will shriek and cower at his sight.

The salt of their souls will bleed, and their eyes will water, flooding down their cheeks".

"He will banish the shamans of the Betan plateau and relegate them to a hundred lifetimes of living among the dirt and the grime, the smog and the ashes, the filth and the decay. For a hundred lifetimes will they wallow in the murky deluge, welter in the muck, and for a hundred lifetimes will they not know the meaning of love, and occupy plague infested bodies, shunned and ignored, dwelling in conditions of extreme poverty without roof or shelter, among animals of the wild".

Almost a week had passed since the Goddess had appeared and in that time the weather had taken a turn for the worse. Babhūti was restless and clambered through the palace like an enraged bull. Across the land dark clouds gathered. Incessant raindrops repeatedly pelted the once fertile fields and the ground became water logged. The crops failed to prosper in soil bogged by sand and muck. The rivers grew deeper and the currents stronger before the dikes finally broke and flooded the valleys and farms.

The air grew colder and the sun vanished. For six days and six nights the tempest raged and the people despaired feeling lost and despondent. They huddled together in their shelters and made sacrificial offerings to the Gods. Animals were slaughtered but fires could not be lit, battered down by a barrage of relentless wind.

Unable to cook the meat they fed on raw carcasses. The nights were dark and gloomy; the chilling cold numbed their bodies. Some resorted to drinking palm wine made from the distilled remains of coconuts and dates; the fearsome liquid scorched their insides but provided their bodies with much needed heat.

Then on the seventh day the storm mysteriously disappeared and the sun was out again. The people rejoiced and Babhūti was back in good spirits. The sunlight cheered him up and after a quick inspection of his kingdom; he made up his mind to do a spot of hunting.

The horses were prepared and the men were readied. Babhūti put on his favorite green hunting gear and as he did so his mind journeyed back in time to when he was a boy. His father, the former king, had taken him on his first hunting trip, deep into the forest, where he had killed his first buck. He was no older than twelve. Babhūti was skilled with the bow. His keen eyesight and unnatural strength gave him the edge over his peers and as a bowman he was unrivalled.

Fully dressed he made his way out of his chamber and kissed his queen on the cheek, bidding her a fond adieu. He made his way towards the stables, in the company of his guards. The sun was out in full splendor and the chorale singing of birds once again filled the air. What a glorious day he thought.

He reached the stables and made for his horse. He stroked the neck of the stallion gently. It was a fine spirited animal, swift, lithe and regal looking. He bought it as a colt almost five years ago. It had cost him handsomely but it was a prudent buy. It was an intelligent beast, with a rare coat of pure white.

He left the stables and rode towards the courtyard where his men were waiting. As they departed Babhūti turned to take a look at his palace before turning away and riding off in search of suitable game. They rode for hours with almost thirty armed men in escort of the king with a pair of scouts riding ahead. They travelled well past lunch without stopping for a break. It was an unusual day for Babhūti; he lacked his normally voracious appetite and rode with uncommon urgency, ignoring the stealth of the hunter and refusing to stalk his prey, choosing instead to stay in the open.

There relentless rain and the barrage of strong winds had altered the landscape tremendously and the serene hills and lush valleys were filled with intermittent lakes and swamps. The unyielding sunshine that followed the rain hardened the ground and life had yet to flourish. The company soon approached a large lake undoubtedly created by the recent rainfall and as they drew closer, Babhūti felt a strange tingle in his hands, like a minute shock caused by the flow of unexpected currents.

The tiny currents spread through his body, racing away to all corners. Babhūti felt giddy, dazed by the sudden surge, and his heartbeat increased twice the norm. He ordered his men to stop and as he jumped off his horse he faltered and almost lost his foothold.

An attendant close to him acted promptly and managed to grab his arm just in time to stop him from falling on the ground. The king steadied himself, ordering his men to set up camp and prepare a meal.

He sat on the mucky floor and inspected the lake. It was filled with flowers, lotuses to be exact, hundreds of them floating indiscriminately on its waters rallying around another much bigger lotus that remained steadfast in the center, the size of a full grown man. A servant handed him a cup of tea and Babhūti accepted it gladly, never for a moment taking his eyes off the giant lotus.

The air was soon filled with the smell of roasting meat prepared with wild herbs and honey. Its enticing aroma drifted through the camp and Babhūti's belly started to rumble. He sat in silence eagerly awaiting his meal.

Once they started eating, Babhūti spoke to the captain of his personal guards who as custom dictated sat close to him. "What do you make of that" he asked, pointing to the giant lotus. The captain paused, unsure of what to say "I'm not sure sire" he replied. Babhūti frowned.

The captain turned his head towards the giant lotus and as they both sat there watching, its huge petals began to unfold. "What manner of magic is this" asked Babhūti aloud. None of his men replied, a bewildered look on their faces. They stared, eyes wide open, gaping in confusing, baffled by the spectacle that was unraveling before them. The petals of the lotus peeled opened one by one to reveal a young boy no older than eight dressed in the meager robes of a monk, sitting in the middle, his eyes closed and his legs crossed.

Babhūti got on his feet and rushed to the banks of the lake and yelled out as loud as he could. Hands cupped around his mouth, he shouted "Are are you all right boy" his voice thundering across the lake, filled with concern. The young boy slowly opened his eyes and a smile lit his face. He replied in a voice that sounded more ominous than crashing thunder. "I'm fine" he said "I'm the glorious Mägi and nothing can hurt me".

Babhūti was taken aback by the abruptness of the boy's reply. Caught off guard he remained silent trying to compose himself, unsure of what to say next. His soldiers looked disconcerted, their uneasy disposition made clear by the blank look on their faces.

Then Babhūti unexpectedly burst out in laughter. He found the boy's manner refreshing. "Come to me boy" he said in a softer non coercive tone. The boy stripped off his robe and jumped into the lake. He swam with ease and within minutes he had reached its banks. He stood up and walked towards Babhūti, stark naked.

The king took a good look at him. His head was bald and his skin was as white as that of the legendary white witch. He had sharpish hawk like features which narrowed down to a well defined jaw. A pointy nose graced his face.

His eyelashes were unusually long and he looked arrogantly becoming. Babhūti was about to say something, when he looked into the boy's eyes. What he saw there made him take a step back. He gasped and took another look but the horror was gone. He could have sworn he saw the reflection of a boar but all that remained were a set of pupils, dark and endless, like the pits of the abyss.

"Well Babhūti?" it was the boy who spoke first. The king was taken by surprise and he stood there, unflinchingly still, trying to gather his thoughts while his guards waited for his instructions. Seconds later, after regaining some semblance of composure, he asked "how do you know my name?" The boy let out a little laugh and replied "I'm the blessed one, Babhūti and I know many things". Silence lingered in the air following the boy's reply. Babhūti's throat went dry and he felt like he needed a drink.

The boy must have read the king's mind because he calmly walked into his tent without being asked and disappeared momentarily before he reappeared, holding an open bottle of wine and a goblet in his hands.

He poured the red wine into the goblet and handed it to the king. The king accepted it gratefully and took a sip. The color returned to his cheeks. Babhūti regained his composure, "get the boy some clothes" he ordered. The veil of silence lifted and the momentary lapse of concentration disappeared. His attendants rushed to find Mägi some clothes. They returned minutes later with the smallest shirt and pants they could find and handed it to the young boy.

Babhūti filled his goblet once more and watched as the boy got dressed. When he had finished Mägi turned to the king, looking like a midget in baggy clothes and said "I have a proposition for you Babhūti". The king's eye brows went up a notch.

"I'm listening" said the king. "You want a son and I can help you". Babhūti was taken aback and the color on his face turned almost as red as the wine he was drinking. He sighed "is there anything you don't know?" he asked. "Not really" replied the boy curtly.

The king couldn't help but smile at the boy's reply. "What is this proposition that you have for me, Mägi?" asked the king. "It's simple" replied the boy. "I'll be your son". Babhūti thought for a moment before nodding his head. He liked the boy. He was certain that his queen would be pleased.

The hunt changed course and took a different route. Mägi took the place of the captain of the royal guards and relegated him to the rear of the column. The young boy had made up his mind to be the king's sole adviser and Babhūti taken in by the boy's wit and manner did not protest preferring instead to observe in silence.

The king had never ventured this far north and as they progressed further the land narrowed bordering Mirkash to the East and the Kingdom of Betan to the north. The winds grew stronger and the journey was often impeded by fallen trees that blocked their passage forcing the company to seek alternative tracks.

The land was sparsely inhabited and they passed many villages with empty wooden dwellings, devoid of human occupants. Most looked deserted and the livestock without human handlers had survived and bred in the wild.

Occasionally they'd spot a flock of sheep or a herd of cattle and Babhūti would do some hunting but the quarry did not present much of a challenge. Unused to humans, the prey stood its ground firmly without taking flight.

The skilled bowman managed to make his kill with a single shot from distances many would hesitate to shoot from. The king was pleased and the company feasted nightly. The scouts were pulled back; Mägi's presence had somewhat increased the king's confidence.

There was something unusual about this land, the sun remained constantly in the sky, towards the west, an orange globe that refused to move or shift. It appeared to be in constant twilight remaining resolutely between day and night. There were no clouds in the sky and a pale orange hue lingered in the air. There was plenty of grass and greenery and flowers were in full bloom but there were no insects. Neither ant nor bee would prospect here. The perpetual wind, displaced all humidity, and the climate was mild to the body.

A week into the journey and the company started to feel uneasy. "What manner of land is this?" asked Babhūti. "It is your neighboring kingdom, Babhūti, you should know it" replied Mägi. "Of course I know it, boy" said Babhūti his tone rising a touch, angered by the boy's bluntness. His outburst was followed by a moment of awkward silence before he decided to rephrase the question. "What I meant was why does the sky remain unchanged, it's unerring, we appear to be no longer in the land of humans" he continued in a much softer tone this time. The boy's mannerisms were abrupt enough to unsettle anyone.

"We're no longer in the land of humans Babhūti". The young monk had taken to calling the king by his first name and Babhūti didn't seem to mind. What you see before you Babhūti is demonic, unending twilight. It is the hour most favored by demons. This land was lost to a demon king many years ago" he continued. "Do you realize why this land is so sparsely populated?" Babhūti shook his head. "It is because most of its occupants have fled in terror" "It is your queen who has thus far shielded your kingdom from the demons".

"Can you make it better?" asked Babhūti. "I can make anything better Babhūti, but you will have to make some sacrifices". "More wine" called out the king, his nerves unsettled yet again, uncertain of what Mägi meant by "sacrifices". He took a swig of the crimson liquid and continued. "I hope you know where we're going?" he asked, his spirits returning. "I always do" replied Mägi.

Babhūti's face turned red again but he remained silent. "Well?" asked the king, after a couple of minutes. "We are going to meet someone". "Why?" he asked, his tone much softer this time. "You'll know when we get there". There was a look of resignation on Babhūti's face. The boy was impossible.

They terrain started to get steeper and the surface of the land altered as they gradually progressed. The greenery thinned to reveal grit and gravel. Black grime clung zealously to the topsoil and dark sediments remained untouched by rain. An uneasy silence filled the air greeted by the sudden disappearance of life. Devoid and destitute the land looked arid. They rode up a hilly track for hours and both horse and men grew increasingly restless as the journey progressed.

They stopped briefly for a meal of cold meat and cider before continuing with their journey. An hour later, they saw the wide open mouth of a cave, hidden and secluded; its rock cut formation synonymous to the Kush Mountains.

As they inched closer they saw a black feminine apparition sitting on a large boulder close to the cave. The specter appeared old and haggard; its body wrapped in faded black cloth and matted locks of thinning white hair hung loosely from its skull, its eyes set firmly on the ground, holding a long wooden staff in one hand. Its skeletal body was clothed with the thinning cover of wrinkled flesh and as they inched closer the rotting stench of decay filled their nostrils.

Mägi signaled for the men to stop. He jumped off his horse and strolled leisurely towards the specter, unperturbed by its grotesque appearance. As he ventured closer, he fell on his knees and took a moment to utter an inaudible prayer. The apparition lifted its head and smiled, betraying a mouth filled with misplaced teeth. It rose from the boulder half bent at the waist and walked towards the cave. Mägi stood up and followed closely behind.

Minutes passed and Babhūti grew apprehensive. His agitated mind began to churn out a range of ominous probabilities. Foremost on the list was the possibility that the boy had fallen into a trap. He was caught up in two minds, unsure of whether to stay or to send in his men to rescue the boy. Just as he was about to decide, Mägi walked out of the cave carrying a sword that almost equaled the boy's height.

The boy strapped the sword to his back, the distance between the bottom of the sheath and the ground a mere inch or two. He seemed unburdened by its weight and as he walked towards the king his face was a picture of serenity. Babhūti was relieved at the sight of the young monk. His mind stopped racing and his pulse returned to normal. He sat patiently on his white stallion and watched as the young boy effortless climbed on to the saddle, adjusting the sword midway. It was an unusual looking sword, unlike anything the king had seen before.

It had a wooden sheath made of dark wood similar to teak, decorated with intricate carvings. Its head resembled that of the might bird of prey Eryr and its handle appeared to be stitched together to the rest of the sword by strands of black thread. Stranger yet was the pommel of the sword or the upper end of the handle which had long flowing black hair attached to it almost reaching to the midway point between the blade and the toe of the sword.

Babhūti gave it a curious look. He was tempted to inquire further but an air of caution swept through him and he bit his tongue. "Who was the hag" he asked. Mägi looked aggrieved. "A Tantric Goddess far more powerful than any you have ever known. Her name is Dhumavati" he said.

"You'd be wise to mind your tongue, Babhūti" he continued. Now it was the king's turn to look aggrieved. He almost went into a fit of rage; his veins expanded twice its normal size and he nearly exploded in anger but sanity prevailed. No one had ever spoken to him in this manner before but if the truth be told he was captivated by the boy's wit and manner.

The ride back was uneventfully. Keen to put as much distance between them and the twilight sun, the company rode at breakneck speed and were soon back in greener pastures. Babhūti was eager to display his prowess with the bow again and he got his chance when they stumbled across a flock of wild sheep. The king called for his longbow made of pure elm.

He selected an arrow from the quiver and was about to place it between the string and the sight window when the young monk stayed his hand. The boy reached for his sword and in one swift singular motion, he lifted it from its sheath and hurled it at the animal farthest from him. The sword traveled at an incredible speed, quicker than the eye could see and plunged into the body of the animal, killing it instantly.

The icy cold winds from the north brought with it sleet and snow and the peaks of the Kush Mountains were an arctic white resembling huge snow cones that sprang from the ground.

The weather altered dramatically and it rained snowflakes. But unlike that of the norm, the icy wafers that blanketed the sky were driven by a dark hand. An age of ice induced by sorcery was about to befall the land. Driven by black magic, the land would freeze and with it all life on the surface. From the pits of the abyss, the fires of hell would be set ablaze, melting away the ice and from beneath the demons will rise.

Farming was abandoned and farmers became trappers and hunters. Children spent their time around warm fires of wood and coal in the company of myths and tall tales, none more entertaining than that of the boar with the golden tusks.

According to legend, at the height of winter, the golden haired princess left her lair in the frozen peaks of the Kush Mountains astride her boar with the golden tusks, each the size of a full grow man, to go in search of anyone lost or abandoned in the snow. If by chance one should stumble upon her, she'd reward them with a bag of gold. It was the dream of every young man in the kingdom to catch a glimpse of the fairy queen and many had gone in search of her only never to return.

The king and queen were pleased with their new son and were content to gradually hand the mantle of leadership over to him. Despite his unusual manner, he was a natural leader. The queen was delighted that she finally had the child that she so desired. She spoilt and pampered him as much as she could. Mägi unable to resist her charms and motherly manner relented.

"Tell me young monk, what is hell like?" asked the queen one day, her curiosity peeked. Mägi smiled, his eyes a blazing red, "Hell is vast; it is endless. It has eight million four hundred thousand precincts in total of which twenty one precincts are the most torturous of the torturous" "I will tell you a little about it" replied Mägi.

"Of hell there is much to say. It is hot, far hotter than the flaming depths of a volcano. The sky above me was red, and the ground below me was crimson. Scarlet was the color of the walls around me. I neither ate nor drank a drop while I was there and watched the rest feast on maggots like mortals do on grains and quench their thirst with the blood of men. The demons are distorted and grossly disfigured in appearance, far more grotesque than any fiend the mind can conjure. Some were gentle in their ways, saddened by their plight".

"My precinct was a thousand furlongs long and a thousand furlongs wide. I confined myself there locked in a state of eternal meditation, the life before forgotten, the life to come unknown. There were very many of them, the hell born, too many to count, marching in hordes, heralded by trumpeters. The quivering notes a warning of the horrors to come. They appeared in all shapes and sizes, twisted and contorted, sharp of tongue and sometimes quick of wit, the keepers of lost souls".

"Those who shared my precinct conformed to a feudal monarchy and were subservient to the hierarchy. Only those in the lower ranks were visible to me. Those higher up in the echelon remained unknown, unseen and unheard. Those that occupied the upper tier of hell were evil but they were bound by the master keeper and were servants of the hellish guardian".

"Of the master keeper I will tell you this. His body is bluish black in color, his neck garlanded by a chain of skulls. He rides a black buffalo and he is armed with a staff, the height of a full grown man. His features reflect the deeds of the beholder, to the good he appears godly and to the evil he appears ghastly. They see what they are. His semblance is but a reflection of their constitution" continued Mägi.

The queen pondered on what she had heard and after a long interval she spoke "Then it is he who you should seek, the master guardian, the keeper of the dead". "Have you by chance spoken to him?" she asked.

The young monk shook his head. "I have merely heard of him. Only the dead spy on his countenance, his visage is unknown to me as is his voice or speech. I am not of the mortal world and unlike mortals I am neither subject to birth nor death. I am the glorious lotus born and I exist untouched by mortality".

"Well lotus born, I command that you to seek the hellish keeper" said the queen, trying to suppress a smile. His manner never failed to amuse her. "Where shall I find him, your highness?" asked the monk his tone equally playful.

"I am surprised that such matters are unknown to a person of your unearthly wisdom" she replied. "Why in the place of the dead of course" she continued.

She stopped briefly before she spoke again, her tone more serious this time. "Immortal you may be but there may come a time when you may slay another. Even as we speak the dark hand of retribution reaches out in search of your soul, for the slaughter of the demons that you are about to unleash. Seek your salvation in the place of the dead lest you be relegated again to another hellish precinct, this time not by choice".

The young monk had changed. His hair reached well below his shoulders but his face remained smooth and beardless. The fire in his eyes had abated and turned into pearls of wisdom. His limbs had paled to become the white of snow; his frame had thinned, he became leaner without any trace of fat. In the years that had gone by his sword had remained faithfully by his side, the strands of black hair that decorated its hilt more vibrant and luxuriant than ever, gleaming in the sun, as alive as he was.

He had left the security of the king's palace to seek restitution for the deaths that he was about to unleash. For five years he meditated unknown to the world in the confines of an obscure graveyard. There he remained feeding on plants and herbs that grew wildly on the ground above the corpses of the dead.

———◆❖◆———

Death is but a transition from one state to another. After death the soul will linger in non existence for a certain period. In that time it can be coerced and it can be cajoled. The will to resist remains while the body rots and the flesh decays.

The spirit of the dead is subjected to the most horrific visions, terrifying drinkers of human blood in different colors, their bodies decorated with skulls and bones, clothed in decaying flesh appear before the spirit. These are called bardo visions. If the spirit can differentiate between the visions, these visions are conjured by its lingering consciousness and reality, than the soul is on the path to liberation or attaining a higher reincarnation. Otherwise it will be reborn in the lower tier of existence.

———◆❖◆———

"Recite the incantations from the Book of Souls to usher the spirit into the afterlife, recite the incantations to stay the spirit in this life or recite the incantations to send it to another life. Trap the spirit to use it for malice or free the spirit to liberate it"

"The wicked spirit is an easy victim; the righteous spirit is a formidable victim. The wicked spirit is malevolent, spiteful and malignant; the righteous spirit is benevolent, kind, and loving. The wicked spirit if it remains stalks the living; the righteous spirit if it remains protects the living. Thus is the perpetual struggle between good and evil prolonged" - Excerpts from the Book of Souls.

Between the pages of The Book of Souls are the secrets of the dead, including the means to control, instruct, and navigate the spirit to do the master's bidding. Be warned that the spirit is at death at varying degrees of strength, the weaker spirit will abide by the master's commands; the stronger spirit will make the master do its bidding. The longer the spirit lingers on earth, the more cunning and devious it becomes, transforming by assuming one shape after another, progressing up the hierarchy, becoming either angelic or demonic.

It was the day of the eclipse and there was silence in the air. Nothing stirred and nothing moved. The day was quieter, calmer and more serene than any other. He heard the distant sounds of tiny bells, little tinkles made by moving anklets. The monk braced himself as the hour approached. The metallic sounds announced the arrival of Maya, the guardian of the dead. Over the horizon there was a faint blur, a bluish speck that grew increasingly larger by the minute, made prominent by two distinguishable horns that swayed left and right on a head that was anything but still.

The face of the animal was black, pitch black to be exact, with a set of eyes that were flaming red with passion and aggression. A water buffalo, in semblance, used to till the fields but larger than any in the known realm. On it was the death God, his bluish black skin, the color of the angry sky, shimmering radiantly in the blazing sun. Wielding a staff that stood taller than any man who walked in his right hand, his neck encircled by a garland of skulls. The beast moved slowly towards the monk.

Mägi's body stiffened as he prepared mentally for the long awaited meeting. The occult born was about to meet a higher source of magic vested with power to unravel the fabrics of the universe.

The sounds of cockleshells announced his arrival, a stark warning of the impending doom. Freed from the abyss below the angel of death heralded his coming, to judge and to mete out punishment if required, as fate had decreed. The eerie silence continued and the winds were stifled. Silence is a sound, audible when all else ceases, it is the hum of the endless ocean, the primeval waters.

The buffalo continued its advance, its rider staring intently at the monk, his lips parting to reveal a smile, gentle, loving, kind and compassionate. The lotus born bowed his head in reverence and sank to his knees. His lips touched the soil before him, a display of servitude; bound by the chains of eternal gratitude. There were twelve before him and he was the last to appear, manifesting at an age when death and destruction were prevalent.

"What is it that you wish for lotus born?" asked Maya, the first to break the silence. "I wish for nothing noble one" the monk replied. The God of Death looked amused at his reply. "Come now Mägi, surely you don't seek me without reason" he said.

The monk nodded his head. "I merely want to be absolved of my sins" he said. The buffalo rider paused momentarily before he spoke. "The cosmic law of action and retribution spares no one and demands satisfaction at all costs". "But you are judged on both your merits and demerits. Therefore for every kill that you make ensure that you save a hundred men and you may be spared" he continued. "It is a simple rule and not beyond mortal or divine comprehension" he added. Mägi nodded his head.

"Tell me most exulted being, of the demons, that come forth, tell me overlord of the demon clan, what is their purpose and what is it that they seek". "Young monk you are still unschooled in the concept of time". "They seek nothing; it is the age of demons, when control of the mortal world is vested in their hands. They seek merely to propagate their demonic ways; like others seek to propagate their godly ways".

Mägi remained silent. "Where is their king o' wisest of beings?" he asked. "In the land across the northern border; he is my disciple and I have gifted him with tremendous powers". "Why, most godly being?" asked the monk. "Because like you thirteenth monk, he too, undertook severe penance to seek my blessings". "You have both been loyal in my worship" he replied.

———⬥⬥⬥———

In the thirteenth year of his mortal existence, Mägi walked out of the graveyard back to the palace of Babhūti and the queen, in solitude. In the time that he was away the land had transformed. Intermittent dots of decay were visible among the once lush fields of green. The odd rotting tree stripped naked of its leaves had become oblivious to the demands of nature. The huts showed signs of dilapidation, nothing unusual but the damage looked more severe than normal. Signs of a slide in fortune, a turn for the worse, were visible everywhere. His eyes recorded all that he saw and stored them like still frames in his mind.

He took a detour traveling first to the north, to demon country where none but the most courageous ventured. It was located inland surrounded by tall mountains. It was almost impossible to forge a living off the rain deserted land and farming was not the preferred occupation. It was more the abode of sages and hermits, monks and priests, witches and wizards.

As he ventured closer towards the desolate terrain, he could see spikes with skulls, embedded in the sun baked soil, protruding upwards from the ground, a warning that he was approaching hostile territory. Carvings in stone became increasingly obvious, representations of meagerly clothed men and women wielding an assortment of weapons, their hair loose and tangled. Depictions of men with heads of animals and tails of lizards, some that he recognized from his time in the world below were etched in stone. Most he decided resembled bardo images.

He had seen enough to make up his mind. Demons plagued this land and its inhabitants were in peril. The dakinis strayed away from this unholy place and the control of the elements became a tussle between them and their demonic adversaries. He turned for home.

"The demon world is feudal and its nation endless, born of demon parents, the infant demon is nurtured like a human offspring. The child demon can be brought into the mortal world and sold into slavery to the black magician, the wizard and the warlock. It is fed with human blood on the night without a moon".

"For twenty nine days the demon is kept in captivity, released on the thirtieth day to feed. It returns to its keeper when the cycle of the moon begins anew. The demon in turn does its keeper's bidding up until the time it outgrows his magic. He who brings the demon into the mortal world is cursed; the act traps his soul within his body and there it remains until the demon is sold or handed over to another willing caretaker"

"Should the owner not hand the demon over to a another before death, his soul stays trapped in his body and at death, when the body rots, he wonders the mortal plane, his soul still intact in his body, a grotesque and contorted carcass, haunting the nights, screaming in anguish and experiencing agony beyond measure, until the death of the demon. The pleasures bestowed by the demon are infinite but the time to indulge in them, finite".

"The demon is a creature like any other, it breeds, it grows, it falls in love and it reproduces. Its lifespan far exceeds that of mortals, but it does perish when its time is up. The demon nation is divided into kingdoms ruled by kings. The demon kings are powerful and none can be subdued by mortal magic. Warring is the demon way, and it is brutal in battle. The demon can die on the battlefield and a demon can be killed by another demon. Demon wars are common"

"The demon society is like the human community, divided into classes, each an expert in its field, the worker demon dominated by the warrior demon, so on and so forth. To control the worker demon is easy; to control the warrior demon is difficult. The higher the status the demon has acquired by birth or by toil the more potent the magic that is required to keep it in shackles. None but the most able sorcerers possess such wisdom and skill"

"The world of the demon coexists with the world of mortals and it is possible for mortals to travel to the world of the demon as it is for demons to travel to the world of mortals.

Should an invitation be extended by the demon king to the mortal, to visit his world, the mortal is blessed"

"The demon is cunning, sly and devious; it seeks to possess the mind and not just the body. It seeks to appeal to the baser instincts of men. The seven deadly sins, pride, covetousness, lust, anger, gluttony, envy and sloth are a means of entrapment and thus does it entice its human victims. The ways of the demon are known to the demon keeper, for that is all a mortal who uses the power of the demon is, a keeper who uses human frailty to fill his purse, granting, boons and wishes, to those who seek his services. The demon can be as pleasing to the eyes or as dreadful to the sight as it wishes. Smooth is its touch, sleek and soft, but firm is its grip, unlike that of any mortal".

"The nation of the demon has but one master, the keeper of the dead and the guardian of hell. The power of hell is the power of three - mortals, the dead and demons" – Extracts from the Book of Demons

Eight years had passed since his return and the climate had taken a turn for the worse. The hazy sun had displaced the radiant light of Shamash. It became a permanent fixture on the horizon and the fertile rays of gold no longer touched the crops. In its place was the tainted light of twilight, its sickly orange rays, swept through the land like a plague.

The air grew cold and the temperatures plummeted. The inhabitants discarded their loose fitting robes and wrapped themselves in thick fur. They started to wither away like jaded roses. The sages disappeared and the hermits vanished, the godly and the wise drifted with the wind and conjurers and sorcerers took their stead.

"They age of the demon is upon us, Mägi, my sisters are losing the battle and the control of the elements shifts to the hands of the demons". "It is time for you to rid the lands of the demons that infest it but it is not a battle that you must undertake on your own" said the queen to the lotus born.

The young monk looked puzzled, "I have my sword with me your highness" he replied somewhat defensively. "Child" chided the queen gently. "Of what use is the sword against the elements?" she asked. Mägi remained silent. The queen continued "You need a companion, someone with the power to move the elements, a dakini like me. It is time for you to take a bride". The silence persisted.

"Nine are the guardians of the Forbidden Mountains, nine are the daughters of the Forbidden Mountains, the power of then ten is vested in the nine; the power of the nine is secured in the one" said the queen. "Who is she?" asked Mägi. "The daughter of Babhūti's nemesis the King of Mirkash" replied the queen.

The monk could say little but nod his head in acknowledgement. "But be warned young monk that once your bond is affirmed by the act of marriage and once it is complete you will depart, never to meet her again in this lifetime".

"A child of your union will merge the power of both and the child will be too powerful. Thus you are both destined to be childless" Mägi sighed there was little he could say, such has Varahi decreed and none could undo her will.

"You will journey to the kingdom of Mirkash, and you will ask for the hand of the king's daughter. The king will consent. He is a noble man loyal to the Goddess. You will leave once the ceremony is over, never to return. Clarity of mind is essential in order for you to complete your task"

The young monk dutifully obeyed the queen's orders and journeyed to the Kingdom of Mirkash and having sought the hand of the king's daughter in marriage, lay silently in his bed anticipating the rite to tie the knot, witnessed by Safa, the most sapient God of Fire. It was a ceremony he would have gladly forgone. Circumstances however demanded obedience and necessity dictated observance. Like everyone else, he too was subservient to the wishes of the Goddess.

The young princess was no older that eighteen, slim, petite, with unusually dark hair that had a purple tinge in it. Her skin was as pale as the snow that covered the peaks of the Forbidden Mountains. Her dark blue eyes sparkled like sapphires with a glint of steel and an unmistakable hint of resoluteness. She was known for her temper that was as uneven as the swirling currents of the sea and her anger that was as blinding as flashes of lightning. Her touch could be as deadly as ice or as fatal as raging flames. Her smile however was as gentle as a summer breeze.

She spoke to the five elements, earth, wind, fire, water and aether. She was a master of the elements and she was rare even among the dakinis. None but few were ever pronounced master of the elements, a title she had acquired years ago.

The elements are more than what meets the eye. They are gateways to other worlds and through the elements, dakinis and other spiritual beings journey from one world to another. Control of the gateways is crucial because it is through the elements that the demon armies and the souls of the death are ferried and transported.

———◈⊰⊱◈———

Lighting set the sky ablaze and peels of thunder roared ominously above. Black clouds of rain blanked out the sun. The tempest raged violently with winds that reached gale like proportions as the young monk prepared for the ceremony in his chamber, the weather a clear indication of his bride's resentment towards the affair.

Mägi hesitated momentarily, as he slipped into the ceremonial attire. The cold air outside was charged with electricity. Never had the monk witnessed such intensity, formulated by a mind with the ability to destroy without moving a single muscle. The strain on the mental faculties must have been enormous.

Their wedding was completed in accordance with custom and tradition. The couple tied the eternal knot of comradeship in the presence of guests and other dignitaries. When the monk touched his new wife for the first time he was thrown back by the currents that drifted beneath her interior. She reached out to him just in time to stop him from being hurled backwards. He felt immense strength in her scraggy limbs.

Her touch was gentle. Mägi smiled at his new wife and instantly understood her tender nature. She was shunned for her gifts, and reviled for her talents. The monk ordered that his wife, Lukina, be taken back to Babhūti's kingdom, there to be mentored by the queen.

Following his marriage and destined to be alone the lotus born ventured north, to the folds of the Kush Mountains. He journeyed only on foot, his faithful sword strapped to his back, across the rugged mountainous terrain, to a nation, stooped deeply in culture and tradition. Dron was the first and foremost religion of the land. There he sought the tutelage of a shaman familiar with the complexities of the Dron faith.

The land was marked with sleet and snow and the hazy sun remained, stagnant over the horizon, reducing the pastures to infertility. It was a land trapped and encircled by white snow conned mountains, isolated and filled with numerous lakes and valleys.

Dron was a religion of rituals, propitiation by means of chants and incantations. It was an antithesis to religious covenants and doctrines complete with a fetishism for sorcery, appraised by the appeasement of spirits and demons, divided between the boundaries of white and black magic.

Mägi enrolled in the house of a known shaman and with his help he acquired knowledge of the Dron religion. Paramount in Dron worship was the Drung or the eight armed cross. It is a key that unlocks the door between worlds and its eight arms represent eight base elements. It is the symbol of perpetual life and growth sustained by the sun.

The founder of the Dron religion Rab - Shen was abducted as a child by the serpent dragon and spirited to the underworld or the netherworld. There under the guidance of the queen of the abyss, who herself like Rab-Shen, was spirited away as a child from the folds of the Sky God, he was taught the ways of spirits and demons. Upon his return he disseminated his teachings, first among family and close friends and then to others who were eager to learn. He was blessed by the queen of the abyss with the ability to control spirits and demons.

He developed an intricate system of rites and rituals to appease and summon both spirits and demons. Dron shamans are able to exert enough control over the spirits and the demons that they summon to make them do their bidding. These spirits can be used to produce either positive or negative results.

The act of appeasement is done with offerings and sacrifices which include fruits, flowers, blood and carcasses. Hence the spirit becomes dependent on the master. It is a faith that is neither good nor evil; it is a faith of achieving a purpose through an earthly means.

Dron is in essence the spiritualism of white and black magic, which can be used for almost any purpose, to perform miracles or bring about mishaps. Rab - Shen nurtured the faith to become a philosophy.

Let there be no doubt as to the power of the Drung. The Gods that it summons are earthly Gods, demons, devils and other entities that reside in the same time and space as mortals, closer to mortals than either the eye or mind can perceive, sometimes within touching distances, sometimes within the shallow casing of the body. Dron is a religion of direct communion.

The Drung opens a doorway between the living and the death, a winding passage with the world of mortals at one end and the abyss at the other. The doorway once opened needs be closed and the spirit once summoned needs to be sent back.

As the faith spread through the kingdom so did the number of spirits that were summoned and upon the death of the Dron shamans, the spirits remained, for many had failed to send them back to the void before their deaths. Spirits and demons of the abyss long outlive their masters. As new spirits and entities were summoned and their masters perished, the dark ones propagated the land and a thousand years after the first summoning, spirits outnumbered humans and in time the demon lord, Samsara, claimed the throne.

The shaman smiled, he neither feared the spirits nor was he disturbed by their presence. He summoned his most powerful spirit to impress the young monk but the spirit failed to appear at the first instance. He was baffled.

He reached for his whip at the end of which was the fruit of a lime tree, fasten with a little knot. He lashed out at the spirit with his whip again. The spirit cried out in pain and anguish and its scream was audible to Mägi but yet again it failed to appear. Angry and frustrated he lashed out for a third time with his whip and the spirit cried out in agony and finally howling in anguish it appeared.

"Why did you not come when you were summoned" asked the shaman. "The spirit clad in white, its body decayed and decomposed, pointed at Mägi and said "I was afraid of the slayer". The shaman looked puzzled and turned his head towards Mägi.

"The wretched wraith speaks but the truth, I am its slayer. I am the slayer of all spirits and demons" said Mägi as he reached for the sword that rested beside him. He drew the blade from its sheath and leapt forward at lightning speed before cleaving the spirit in half and instantly freeing the abject soul. "What manner of magic do you use slayer" asked the shaman. "Tell about your magic" he continued. Mägi nodded his head.

"I am a Tantric, noble shaman" he replied. "The Tantric teaching moves within riddles and circles. It is first and foremost the faith of knowledge and with knowledge alone will the riddles be solved, without knowledge the body will be trapped in an endless circle"

"Faith without knowledge is blind faith; faith without practice is no faith. The Tantric faith like yours is a faith of direct communion; it is the faith of circles within circles. It is the faith of perpetual motion".

The shaman composed himself "a hundred and one days have you stayed with me and a hundred one secrets have I bequeath to you, but you have hidden your true self from me". "Are you a more powerful shaman than I" mocked the shaman. "Have you forgotten that I am your teacher, surely your abilities pale in comparison to mine" he continued.

"Noble shaman, your knowledge is but a drop in the Tantric sphere and your ability to reason is restricted by your pride. I am born of occult and occult I am. I am occult in its entirety" replied Mägi.

The shaman's face turned red with anger, his heart pounded faster than normal. Fury clouded his judgment. Blinded by rage he lashed out at the monk with his whip. Mägi sidestepped the attack with ease and slapped the air around him. His blow landed on the cheek of the shaman who was standing at least ten feet away from the monk and threw him clear across the wooden hut. The shaman landed flat on his back, drops of blood oozing from his nose and ears. His spirit drifted out of his body and Mägi heard its loud shrieks as it came in contact with the other spirits that he had so tormented. The languishing scream disappeared gradually as it was dragged into the void.

Mägi stepped out of the hut sword in hand and as he walked out he could see black spots moving on the ground, footsteps, dispersing at incredible speed, as fleet as wind. "He opened his third eye and he could see the spirits of the dead. They whispered to each other of the coming of the slayer and shuddered like leaves on a tree.

The Betan Plateau

At the age of twenty one Mägi journeyed back to Betan where he had met Dhumavati many years ago. The pale orange sky turned an ominous grey and black clouds appeared across the sky for the first time in years as he approached. The battle for the elements had begun. Control of the elements was essential to wrest the kingdom away from the clutches of the demon king.

Lighting flashed before the monk as he ventured forward. It was a sinister attempt at intimidation but Mägi scorned at the effort and treated it with contempt and disdain. A second blaze of lighting shot like an arrow through the air. It struck the monk but he was not unsettled by the attack. The black clouds retreated shoulders shrugged in defeat.

The monk journeyed for weeks, slaying any demon or spirit in sight. He visited the Dron shamans and spread his teachings. He taught them his way, the Tantric way and altered their way of thinking. He amended the rituals and put a fresh spin on existing customs. He merged the faiths, the old faith with the new and created a unique fusion of religions. He forbade the enslaving of spirits, which was prevalent in Dron rites and shared with his new found disciples his knowledge of the dead.

His wisdom was condensed into words and his teachings which became Betan's most prized treasures were hidden in lakes and mountains away from prying eyes and thieving hands. He opened the hearts and the minds of the people.

The malicious spirits that freely roamed the land were relegated back to the astral world, to the realm between the world of the living and the world of the dead. The demon king angered by the demise of his ghostly legions sought the counsel of Maya.

"Do not send your warriors to battle the glorious lotus born but send instead your daughter the lovely Princess Niemi. He is too strong for the hell spawns. Tell her to ensnare him not with her might but with her charms. Where the sword has failed the heart might prevail" counseled the keeper of the dead.

So eager was the demon king to defeat Mägi that he instantly sped off in search of his daughter failing to hear the last sentence. "Take heed demon king, should she fail, all is lost".

The Princess Niemi was tall in frame, lean of body and blessed with whipcord strength and a swordsman's tan. She had long ebony black hair which reached down below her shoulders and her eyes were the color of dark pearls. Her forehead was wide, a common trait among the demon blood and her jaws narrowed to complete the devilish structure of her face. All in all she was enchantingly pretty. She towered in height well above the others and was ruthless in her pursuits and relentless in battle.

Niemi upon hearing her father's instructions sat astride her black stallion and journeyed in search of the lotus born. Horse and rider travelled swiftly and navigated skillfully through the mountainous terrain. Her stallion moved at tremendous speed, its long legs took huge strides and it covered vast distances in half the normal time. The hell bred stallion, breathed smog and fire and a fierier beast was nowhere to be found.

Far away in Babhūti's palace the queen and Lukina looked into a crystal ball in the privacy of the queen's chamber and they saw Niemi go in search of the monk. They combined their powers and summoned clouds of rain to obstruct the orange sun and slow her down. The land was pelted with drops of water falling from the skies and hail came crashing down from above.

Lukina whose control over the elements was unprecedented, ruthlessly defeated the demons who sought to thwart her efforts, burning them with flashes of lighting and reducing them to cinders, leaving their ashes to scatter in the wind but the acolytes of the demon king were resourceful and even as one disappeared another emerged to take its place. It put a huge stain on Lukina's energies and sapped the pair but the women were resolute in action and refused to yield in battle, their will unbending.

Mägi was caught unaware. He was with a group of fresh disciples when the weather took a sudden change for the worse. With his third eye he spied on the queen and his wife and saw the coming of Niemi. He studied her features from afar and realized that she was of the demon blood.

He found her appealing but he didn't allow passion to cloud his judgment. He knew the reasons for her coming. He dismissed his students and prepared for battle. He sat in silent meditation contemplating the events to come. Mägi relished the prospect of facing an enemy that was competent. Thus far no one had surpassed him in a dual and he was hoping that Niemi may offer him a challenge.

Despite being told to seduce the young monk, the princess, was overcome by the lust for battle and was overly confident of her abilities with the sword. Her father's proposal seemed infinitely complex and time consuming. It was just easier to decide the matter with a swift stroke of the blade.

She rode tirelessly for a week, resting only on short intervals for meals and sleep. She journeyed across the rugged uneven terrain with skill few could muster and at the end of the week she had managed to locate Mägi. She found him seated at the mouth of a cave, legs crossed, sword strapped to his back, in full meditation.

She jumped off her stallion as soon as she caught sight of him and rushed at him, her sword clear from its sheath, raised well above her head, held high in her right hand. Just as she was about to strike, the lotus born nimbly moved away and managed to avoid the premeditated stroke with ease. He pulled his sword from the sheath that protected the blade and looked into her eyes. She met his gaze with a steely glare.

Niemi hurled a teasing blow but the lotus born remained steadfast, unperturbed by the attack. His defense was restrained and he curbed his aggressive nature aware of the lethal damage his sword could do. Niemi hesitated, her spirits sinking slightly at the failure to detect fear. She moved like a caged lioness, her stance menacing and her posture hostile as she waited for the monk to retaliate. Mägi refused to attack and as they stood there looking at each other, the anger slowly dissipated and in its stead, stood two confused combatants.

The demoness was the first to speak. "Why have you come?" she asked. "To free your people" replied the lotus born. They are enslaved by sorcery and bonded by magic, tormented by the souls of the dead who seek revenge and retribution". "The land and its occupants will wither and fade away like jaded flowers. The evil will spread to neighboring kingdoms and infest their lands with malevolence". "Let me cure you of the demon ailment that plagues you and you will be forever free, unhindered and untainted by the nemesis of good".

The demoness stood still with her head held high and pondered over what she had just heard before she gradually let her guard down. The monk walked up to her. He placed his thumb on her forehead and absorbed the rage from within. The anger soon abated and the fury subsided. She felt calm, freed at last from the shackles that had held her captive since birth.

Back at the palace the queen and Lukina watched the turn of events and withdrew their attack on the demons. They were drained and sapped from the effort but it was not in vain. They had managed to weaken the demon horde.

"Will you show me the way to your palace" asked the monk. Niemi nodded her head. She took him by the hand and they rode back together on her horse to the palace of the dreaded demon king Samsara and his consort Mara.

Unlike an ordinary demon, the demon king, like the lotus born was eternal untouched by the cycle of birth and death. He had eight heads on his shoulders, each facing a separate direction, and he had eight arms on his body each wielding a different weapon.

His skin was as black as tar, smooth and faultless, harder than steel. No man could stand against him and his strength was a threat even to lesser deities.

His consort Mara was the eternal seductress. She tempted the hearts of men with her unparalleled beauty. Her lips were luscious, the red of rubies, her eyes the green of glowing emeralds, her skin impeccably fair and her body perfectly proportioned. She was the bearer of a special boon and any man who looked into her eyes would instantly lose his heart to her.

The palace of Samsara and Mara was black the color of pitch. As the pair approached, the hazy sun remained unmoved in the background; its pale orange light illuminating the way. It was on a clear day that they rode to the abode of the demon king. The air was still, nothing stirred and nothing moved. The monk opened his third eye and he could see the demonic rituals that were taking place behind the four walls.

Demons like humans were subservient to Gods; they worshipped the hellish guardian and like humans performed rites and rituals with piety and fidelity that far surpassed that of any mortal, the demon king more so than others. They were unmatched in reverence and far outdid humans in the worship of the omnipresent and the omniscient. They were faultless in their obeisance and veneration. Apart from their appearance they were flawed only in one aspect, in that they tried to usurp the Gods. Initially they were granted power beyond measure but they were robbed of their power when they rebelled.

The power of the demons is not beyond humans. Their rites are written in sacred texts and any mortal who strictly observes these rites will obtain the power of demons. Any mortal who abuses the power will be stripped of it and relegated to the extreme end of the reincarnation cycle.

Demonic power is perverse and it will corrupt humans in totality.

The palace gates swung open and as they entered the sounds of demonic worship grew increasingly audible. The alphabet "S" was prominent in the demon tongue and their speech was sibilant. The courtyard looked deserted with the exception of the odd hooded figure, clocked in brown tunic, going about its business. It looked empty to the naked eye but to the third eye it was filled with spirits lurking around every corner.

The monk touched the base of Niemi's spine with his index finger and his actions opened her third eye. She was instantly granted sight beyond sight. She swung into action almost immediately after she had acquired her outer vision. Sword in hand; she cut and hacked indiscriminately at anything that moved. The air was filled with screams of terror. Her assault was brutal and she was unwavering in her chastisement.

The noble lotus born reached for the sword that was strapped to his back. He withdrew it from the sheath and it gleamed at the prospect of cleansing its metal with blood. He joined in the carnage and soon the courtyard was filled with demonic remains, scattered indiscriminately on the ground. The pair fought together side by side until they reached the throne room. The monk kicked the door opened, it shattered at the force of his blow, to reveal Samsara and Mara seated on the thrones, beside each other.

Niemi dropped to one knee at the sight of her parents and she withdrew from battle out of sheer respect. She could not attack the demon king and his consort. The demon king rose from his throne and reached for an amulet, a miniature drung that hung from his neck.

He tugged at it until it became loose and tossed it on the ground in front of him. The drung started to swirl in circular motions increasing in circumference, growing larger with each passing minute, turning at incredible speeds, before finally stopping to unveil a circle of fire. The demon king jumped into the blazing circle and raised his eight arms in readiness for battle.

The monk watched the events that transpired and understood the nature of the flaming circle. It was a defensive perimeter, an invisible wall protected by sorcery, beyond the reach of ordinary magic. Mägi summoned the help off the queen and Lukina. Having recovered sufficiently from their previous battle, the women agreed.

The dakinis unleashed strong winds from eight directions, carrying with it drops of water. There was a consequent battle between the flames of demons and the raindrops of the dakinis.

The flames flickered and floundered, smothered by the rain drops. As soon as he saw the flames subside Mägi leapt into action and hacked away furiously at the demon Samsara, his initial thrust cleaving an outstretched arm off the demon, severing it from its body. It fell into the now docile flames, and the limb of the demon was reduced to cinders by the very flame that was conjured to protect it.

The monk moved swiftly around Samsara whose defenses were easily breached and the demon's armored skin was cut by the magical sword of the monk. The demon bled profusely, green liquid oozing out of its body and it screamed in pain. The ground trembled at the sound of its voice. One by one the monk hacked off the arms of the demon until none remained.

The demon jumped around in pain and anger while Mägi waited for the appropriate moment. When it presented itself, he lashed out at the necks of the demon with his sword cleaving the heads clean off its shoulder. The heads and body fell into the dying flames and were reduced to ashes. The demons that sought to control the elements instantly retreated at the demise of the demon king. Samsara disappeared into the endless void, the sound of his mocking laughter reverberating across the land.

Samsara could never be destroyed only thwarted; the scourge of mankind was as eternal as its savior. The hazy sun vanished and the golden rays of Shamash came streaming through the holes on the walls that were caused by the battle that had unfolded. The golden light touched the skin of Mara, the demon queen, scalding it badly and she screamed in pain and agony. The monk spared her and relegated her to a fate worse than death, to remain the ghostly seductress who shunned the sun for all eternity".

The monk reigned for a thousand years and spread his teachings across the kingdom. He founded schools that sprung like wild mushrooms across the land and disseminated his faith.

Neither the dead nor the living were ever tormented again and all beings mortal and celestial coexisted in peaceful harmony for a thousand years. In the thousandth year after his appearance the monk, Lukina and Niemi disappeared without a trace, never to be heard from again but the lotus born left behind a promise that he will return at the appointed time.

Of his return it is said that a glass casket will appear from the sky and within it he will be asleep dressed in white garments made from the purest cotton. The casket will drift to the ground and the glass lid will slide open. On the day of his return, his army will be ready to greet him, dressed in white.

Printed in the United States
By Bookmasters